AUDREY
(COW)

*An oral account of a most daring escape,
based more or less on a true story*

DAN BAR-EL

ILLUSTRATED BY

TATJANA MAI-WYSS

TUNDRA BOOKS

Published in Canada by Tundra Books, a division of Random House of Canada
Limited, One Toronto Street, Suite 300, Toronto, Ontario M5C 2V6

Published in the United States by Tundra Books of Northern New York, P.O. Box
1030, Plattsburgh, New York 12901

Library of Congress Control Number: 2013953683

Library and Archives Canada Cataloguing in Publication

Bar-el, Dan, author
Audrey (cow) : an oral account of a most daring escape, based more or less on a
true story / by Dan Bar-el ; illustrated by Tatjana Mai-Wyss.

Issued in print and electronic formats.
ISBN 978-1-77049-602-6 (bound).–ISBN 978-1-77049-604-0 (epub)

I. Mai-Wyss, Tatjana, 1972-, illustrator II. Title.

PS8553.A76229A83 2014   jC813'.54   C2013-906922-4
                                            C2013-906923-2

Edited by Tara Walker and Debbie Rogosin
Designed by Andrew Roberts

The artwork in this book was rendered in watercolor and pencil on recycled
Bristol. The cover artwork was rendered in watercolor and colored pencil on
Rives BFK paper.
The text was set in Georgia.

www.tundrabooks.com

Printed and bound in the United States of America

1 2 3 4 5 6   19 18 17 16 15 14

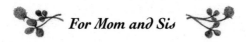 *For Mom and Sis*

We peck and scratch out our earthly days,
but how we long to fly.
How we long to fly.

— Lulu Belle, *Memoir of a Rhode Island Red*

MADGE
(cow)

How would I describe her in a word? Well . . . young. That was her, plain and simple. Too young to go through what she did, poor thing.

EDDIE
(dog)

Gosh, I'd have to say kind. She was really kind. And sweet too! That's two words, isn't it? May I use two words? Because I would have to say she was both really kind and really sweet and beautiful too. Ah, heck, that just came out! Can we cut that part? Please? Everyone is going to give me a razzin' for that!

GRETA
(cow)

In vun verd? Tragic. (*sniff*) Ya, tragic is a good verd.

NORMA
(cow)

Pass! . . . What? Oh, for heaven's sake. No, *pass* is not my word to describe her! I meant that I was not taking part in this silly interview. She's gone. Out of sight, out of mind, I say.

ROY
(horse)

I reckon I'd have to say plucky. She was a pretty l'il thing, but underneath that soft hide was one brave gal.

BUSTER
(pig)

Obviously, the word would be *vacca* . . . Why? Because that's Latin for cow. Oh dear, oh dear, oh dear, I hope you brought along some harder questions.

AUDREY
(cow)

How would I *briefly* describe myself? I'm afraid I am not a cow of few words. Mother once said that my heart speaks

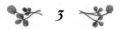

a mile a minute, by which she meant that emotions can get the best of me, and then I'm off to the races, conversation-wise. It was her suggestion that I practice distilling my feelings into fewer words. But as to your question . . . hmm. How can you describe anyone, really? The inside and outside can be so different. Here is a poem I composed a while back, near Artificial Lake, around the time of my awakening. It goes like this:

> *The cow that I spied was silent and still*
> *Her smile serene, her mood tranquil*
> *Oh, to be she, without worry or fear*
> *Empty of dread and full of good cheer*
> *Familiar she seemed and on closer inspection*
> *It was me that I spied in the water's reflection*

So you never really know, do you? But I think that if I was to choose just one word to describe myself, that word would be *alive*. Yes, *alive*. You see, I knew exactly where I was, and I knew exactly where I was heading, which was downhill, straight to the meat section of the supermarket. That just

wasn't acceptable to me. I mean, I had dreams. I wanted to go places . . . *other* than to the meat section of the supermarket. I wanted to taste new grasses and flowers and see a million sunrises and sunsets. I had no time for cows who said, "Audrey, this is your lot in life. Accept it and make the best of it." I couldn't. I couldn't give up on life so soon.

GLENN

(human)

Again? It seems the interest in Audrey won't ever settle down. What more can I tell you folks? The truth is that this whole media hullaballoo is embarrassing. Bittersweet Farm has been in my family for four generations. We're not particularly big. We're certainly no factory farm. We have a variety of animals, but cows are a big part of the business. Audrey was born here. As far as I know and understand cows, I would not say that Audrey was special. But I will admit she was memorable. I'd often have to send my older dog, Max, out to the far end of the property to bring her back to the barn. But I didn't discover any half-dug tunnels under the fence, like they've been saying on television. That just didn't happen.

As for what *did* happen, I have no comment. Look, we brought her mother onto the farm as an experiment. A new breed we were trying out. Maybe it didn't take. Maybe that was what made Audrey do what she did. Not to sound corny, but I always felt that we all got along on Bittersweet Farm—all of us. There were no hints that something was amiss.

AUDREY
(cow)

My breed? Why, I'd be happy to tell you. I'm a Charolais. It kind of rhymes with parlay, which is how you would say "to speak" if you said it in French. France is where my roots are, in the town of Charolles, which is in the middle of the country. I know all this partly from Mother but also from Little Girl Elspeth, who was showing off to her city cousin. She had a book in her hand and was pointing to a map, and I was spying over their shoulders. That's how I learned about the land of my ancestors. That's also where I learned about the giant lake called Atlantic that separates Bittersweet Farm from France and that brought my dream of travel to a halt. You see, I wanted to visit Charolles and partake of the local food. Little Girl Elspeth showed pictures in her book of French Charolais—my cousins, I suppose. They were standing in fields, grazing on flowers that I did not recognize. They looked delicious, the flowers, I mean.

ELSPETH

(human)

Audrey . . . she was my favorite. I could talk to her. I could, you know. Audrey was always nice . . . she would listen . . . *I* think she was special.

AUDREY

(cow)

We Charolais, you will note, are all white—but creamy white would be more accurate. We don't have those black splotches that you find on similar-looking white breeds. Norma says the black splotches give her character and uniqueness. She says it makes her interesting, implying that Charolais are not. But Mother said that Charolais come into the world as blank canvases and our potential is unknown at first.

Mother said that my character would be painted on the inside. I like that. Whenever I experience something that makes me happy—if I hear a robin singing just before dawn or if I inhale the scent of grass just after a rainfall— I imagine that the tickling I feel inside is a paintbrush dabbling on another splotch of my uniqueness. I was strengthened by thoughts like that, especially in the face of what others were telling me—others who were far less generous. For example, the book from which Little Girl Elspeth was reading that day said that Charolais are docile by nature, which means we're quiet and easy to control.

It means that we're unlikely to cause any trouble. Well, you can decide for yourself how true that observation turned out to be.

NORMA

(cow)

Oh, that Audrey, she was born with fancy pants on, that one. What? Yes, I know perfectly well what I said earlier! I'm not senile, and I'm not a dim lightbulb like Agnes either! Everyone knows I'm not one to gossip, but if you're going to insist on telling this story, you'd better have at least one cow who can give you the facts. First time out of the barn, Audrey was talking about going to the farthest fields and tasting this grass or that clover, or maybe talking to a passing fox. Imagine, talking to a common thief! I'd been here a lot longer than she had, but I never ventured past the first hill. And why should I? Plenty of grass nearby—who needs to go farther? That's the kind of reckless behavior that comes from a wild upbringing, not that I like to judge.

I didn't care much for Audrey's mother when she arrived. It wasn't that she was rude; on the contrary, she was very refined, and quietly so. Not show-offy, which I, naturally, wouldn't stand for. Come to think of it, I don't know why we didn't become closer. She was different, you understand. Her family roots were . . . well, let's just say she wasn't from around here. For one reason or another, we never spent much time together. She always seemed to be grazing at the opposite end of the field, and with my weak ankles, I just wasn't . . . it doesn't matter anyhow. In hindsight, it was all for the best. I certainly couldn't condone her parenting style. Look at how her daughter turned out!

GRETA

(cow)

Audrey vas a dreamer. It is not lie. She vas too delicate for this harsh vorld of farm, ya? I know, for I too vas like a delicate daisy. But in time, life vill shape you into something stronger and more resilient. It can be painful, ya, but vat choice do ve have?

MADGE

(cow)

Greta said what? My goodness, that cow could spin a tragedy out of a mosquito bite. The only horrible thing to happen to Greta was she once missed a morning milking and didn't get any relief for a few extra hours. But there is some truth to what she said. As far as us cows are concerned, our lot in life is decided before we come into the world. And I said exactly that to Audrey when the time came. I said to the girl, "Audrey, there are but three kinds of cows. There are milk cows, like me. There are work cows, like old Betty. And then there are food cows, and I'm afraid that your destiny is to be dinner." It was harsh, I admit, but the poor dear needed to know the facts, plain and simple.

She heard me, but she wasn't really listening because . . . well, Audrey was special. And I mean that in a good way, not like how Greta and Norma and all the other gossiping ninnies mean it. Audrey reminded me of Lon, my son, whom I miss greatly to this day. They're both made of the same sparkly cloth, if you catch my meaning. Both looking up at the moon and believing it's within their grasp, that *anything* is within their grasp if they desire it enough. If you ask me, that's the real tragedy. Cows and steers meant for the dinner table shouldn't be curious or filled with wonder. They should be boring creatures who spend their days looking at the trough or the tail in front of them.

AUDREY
(cow)

Oh, I remember absolutely everything about the day Madge told me what would become of me. I had just composed another poem, this one paying tribute to some delicious clover I had recently discovered on the southern slope of Viewing Hill. It went:

> *Clover green, a tasty treat*
> *I'm grateful for each one I eat*

I was sharing the poem with my best friend, Eddie, and telling him about my plans to visit the land of my ancestors and tour the countryside, tasting all the grasses and clover the region has to offer.

Eddie was great. He never laughed at my plans, not like most of the cows in the barn. And I did hear them laughing, even though I pretended not to. I know they thought I was oblivious, but I assure you I wasn't. I heard all the snickers and Norma's hoof-scraping whenever I walked by. But Madge wasn't like that. She wasn't what I would call friendly or anything, but you always knew where you stood with Madge.

I heard she lost a son—had him taken away from her, and she was just supposed to get over it because it happened all the time on the farm. But I don't think she did, and I don't blame her. I think Madge lost a part of herself, a part of her heart, maybe. Don't ask me how I know because it's not a knowing kind of thing. A mist of sadness is how I'd describe it. Yes, a mist like we'd get on gray, foggy mornings that made the farm seem as if it were fading away along its edges. That's what it was like with Madge, the sadness hovering around *her* edges, threatening to fade *her* away.

So I knew Madge was coming over to Eddie and me even before I turned my head and saw her. I could feel the sad

mist. Then Madge told me what I needed to know, told it to me straight . . . about the three types of cows . . . and how I was in the least favorite category.

EDDIE

(dog)

I was there! Jeepers, it was awful! Audrey's eyes grew big, really big, as big as Buster's eyes get whenever his slop pail is empty and he realizes there's nothing left to eat. At first Audrey didn't say a thing. She was as quiet as a windless night, and gosh, I got a little scared myself! I stood up on my hind legs so I could reach high enough to give Audrey a few licks on her chin. She likes that, and aw, heck, it doesn't mean we're boyfriend and girlfriend or anything, okay? It's just something I do to make her happy, in the same way that Audrey licks my face whenever Dad gives me a chewing out for making another mistake. But poor Audrey, she was not consoled. She said to me, "Oh, Eddie, what's going to happen to me? I don't want to be a food cow. Whatever will I do?" It made me want to howl, because I didn't want Audrey to be a food cow either. She looked so sad, and I'm sure at that moment she was probably thinking she'd never get to France to taste all those delicious grasses and flowers. And that's when I told her not to worry, we'd figure something out. But there was no plan at that time. No sirree. No plan at all.

ROY

(horse)

The plan? Whoa, now hold on there, partner. Yer jumping the story ahead of itself, putting the cart in front of the horse. Before you start chasing Audrey's tale, you might want to bide a moment and consider Jeanine, Audrey's mother. Jeanine is the key to this here adventure. It all started with her.

AUDREY

(cow)

Mother and I didn't have long together, but I will always remember every precious second. Mother was very smart and beautiful. She was kindhearted too. There was a glow that shone around her. It's true; I saw it. When I was just a little heifer, I'd study her sitting beneath an oak, all at peace, her eyes dark and shiny, and a halo of light radiating all around her. Mother's voice was soft, and she never spoke quickly. "Audrey," she might say to me one morning, "look at the sun breaking beyond the hills. Isn't it beautiful? Can you feel the rays starting to warm your body? Can you see the shadows falling away? Feel the dew on your hooves, cool and wet. In a couple of hours most of it will be gone, but you'll find drops hugging the grass and moistening your tongue as you graze. Dew drop surprises!"

Mother was what some might call a detail cow, I suppose, because she'd notice the smallest parts of life—parts that most other cows skip over. I have a different name for her, though. As much as I respect Madge and appreciate her looking out for me since Mother went away, and giving me the facts straight as she did, I do believe that she was mistaken in one regard. There may be work cows and milk cows and food cows, but there is also another type. There are poet cows, and they too serve a purpose. My mother was one such cow. She could describe the world in all its beauty, separating the harsh and ugly parts like farmers separate the wheat from the chaff. With her words, she made the world golden and tasty and so very big, but not scary.

Yes, Mother was a poet cow. And I had to believe that, as her daughter, I might have inherited some of those same qualities. If so, surely I was meant for something more than a truck ride to Abbot's War.

NORMA
(cow)

You want to know about WHAT? Shame on you! Cows don't talk about Abbot's War. It's considered a very impolite subject to bring up among decent company. Goodness gracious, it gives me shivers just thinking about it.

GRETA
(cow)

Ya, it's true, so true! Abbot's Var is best left unspoken (*sniff*) for it vill only bring deep and terrible sadness.

AGNES

(cow)

Oh, that? Heck, I don't mind talking about
Abbot's War. It's like a mystery, eh? And
I like mysteries! (*snort*) I like watching grasshoppers too and saying
"whacka-whacka" over and over,
and I like science fiction and stuff
that's gross (*snort*)—which everyone
says I should keep to myself, so I will.
But mysteries are at the top of my list of
favorite things. Mysteries rock! Abbot's War is not a good
kind of mystery, though, like the mystery of how a new calf
can get on her legs an hour after birth, which is a beautiful, glorious miracle of life but also kind of gross, 'cause
she's all covered in slimy goo, eh? Oops. (*snort*) Sorry.
And it's not a happy mystery either, like why humans keep
wanting to exchange food for our milk. They do, you know!
This arrangement has been going on for years and years!
What's that all about? (*snort*) But Abbot's War is a dark,
unsettling mystery, like how the chickens keep clucking

about their disappearing eggs. Whoa! Lots of weird stuff happens on a farm, eh?

EDDIE
(dog)

You bet I'll tell ya, but I'm warning you it isn't nice, no sir-ree. See, a truck comes to the farm every so often, and a few select cows are loaded in it. They never return. That's what happened to Madge's son, Lon. That's what happened to Audrey's mom too. We overheard Farmer and his family refer to the truck's destination as Abbot's War. None of us know what a war is, but the cows are convinced that it isn't great.

Jeepers, I never told any cow what I'm about to tell you, so it has to remain a secret, okay? There's a smell on that truck, and, gosh, it's horrible. It's not strong, but it's definitely there. I asked Dad what it was once, and he got very serious. He looked around to make sure no one was within earshot before he spoke. Then he said in a quiet growl, "Son. That is the stench of death. Do not forget that smell because if it leads you to a sheep from the herd you were responsible for, it means you weren't doing your job. As for the smell on the truck, you keep that knowledge to yourself, you hear? Farmer doesn't need his cows spooked."

AUDREY

(cow)

I knew what Abbot's War was. We all knew, all of us: the cows, the sheep, the chickens and even Buster. There wasn't any mystery about it, except maybe for Agnes, but then a lot of things are a mystery for Agnes. It's just that . . . no one wanted to know. Everyone pretended it was a mystery because it's so hard to accept that life can be so precious and so fragile at the same time. I'm not one to judge, because when Abbot's War suddenly became personal, I too chose to pretend ignorance.

As for Mother, she knew where she was going. She heard it directly from the horse's mouth. Roy always finds out first. Given a choice, you'd want to hear it from Roy because he brings solemn dignity to the announcement. That's how Mother put it. Roy doesn't gloat, and he isn't caught up in feeling relief because it's you and not him. Roy looks you in the eye and whispers the hard facts, but he isn't cruel. Mother said that through his sturdy gaze, Roy could give you the courage to bear the news and not have your four legs collapse beneath you as if a carpet of moss was being pulled away beneath your hooves.

EDDIE

(dog)

Darn tootin', I like Roy. Everyone likes Roy! Well, maybe Dad doesn't. That's because Roy doesn't really do any work on the farm. But I heard that he used to work on a ranch in the Rocky Mountains way back, and he did cattle drives. Gosh, that's pretty swell. Now he's retired. He's the family horse, and he can go wherever he pleases on the property. He's allowed to poke his head through the kitchen window if there's food to be mooched. I mean, I know how to mooch too! But jeepers creepers, if it's Middle Boy Lester handing out the treats, I have to put some effort into it, getting on my hind legs and dancing around or rolling on my back. I don't do that with Little Girl Elspeth, no sirree, because she'll just pat my head or rub my belly. But Roy, he only has to come over to say hello, and bingo, he's getting sugar cubes or carrots or apples. Ah, heck, I'm not jealous. Roy performs a big service for all of us. By timing it right, Roy can duck his head in during Farmer family mealtimes and pick up useful information.

ROY

(horse)

Heh, heh, heh, oh, I reckon I am a tad spoiled. Good food, comfortable stall, not many riding duties other than Little Girl Elspeth, and she don't weigh more than a flea. Not like some of them city slickers I used to haul up and down the mountainside. So I'm mighty grateful for this ease in my senior years. I do like my sugar cubes, and I love a shiny, red apple now and then, but otherwise, I try not to get underfoot.

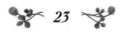

And I try to offer some service to the others. Max wouldn't see it that way, but Max takes his job a little too seriously, in my opinion. I'm the farm newspaper, you could say. I keep my ears open to the human conversations and pass on information to whomever might find it pertinent. Buster always wants to be reassured that his corn feed has arrived. In spring, the sheep are desperate to know when they'll finally get to lose their heavy wool coats. And with the food cows . . . well . . . let me put it this way: in my life, I've seen my share of tragedy. I've seen horses hurt out on the trail that never got to say final good-byes to loved ones. So if I am privy to information that could give a parent a chance to say what needs to be said before heading off to Abbot's War, then, by golly, I will pass it on.

Not everyone wants to know, mind you. Some see me coming and head in the opposite direction. Shoot, some-times I wasn't even going to talk to them. I was just strolling toward Viewing Hill to see what the neighbors were up to. Most are grateful, though. They might be a tail-swat away from fainting at the time, but they still want to prepare. But Jeanine, Audrey's mom, she didn't flinch. And after I told her what I had heard, about the truck arriving the next day around noon and that she was on the list . . . Jeanine thanked me. Yes, she did, as graciously as if I had wished her a good day. She nodded and smiled and went to find her daughter. She was quite a lady.

AUDREY

(cow)

Mother came to me shortly after she heard. She didn't seem any different than usual. She wasn't nervous or weepy the way Greta gets. She was her usual radiant, peaceful self. I was playing with Eddie. Well, playing isn't the best description. Eddie can get so wound up and excited that I can barely keep him in sight as he darts all around me. But Mother came over and asked him if he would please excuse us because she wanted to talk with me privately. Poor Eddie. He probably thought he did something wrong. His tail was all tucked in when he left.

"Stroll with me, Audrey," Mother said. "Let's head over to the grove. It's been a while." I didn't suspect anything at first. But when Mother started talking, her topic of

conversation was surprising. She told me that among cows there is an oral history of feats accomplished by cows in the past. These stories have somehow managed to be passed from farm to farm, from region to region and even across national borders. "You mean like France in Europe on the other side of the lake called Atlantic?" I asked. I could tell Mother was impressed with my knowledge because she took a moment to beam at me with pride, and I basked in her smile like it was summer sunshine.

Then Mother proceeded to give me an example. "Yvonne of Bavaria managed to jump over an electric fence and onto a busy country road. They say she stared down a car until it screeched to a halt, and then, as casual as a Sunday promenade, Yvonne continued to the other side and into a thicket of trees." I was astounded. A cow jumping over a fence? I had no idea we were capable of that. "So what happened to Yvonne?" I asked Mother. "They say Yvonne was never seen again," she replied. Let me repeat that, at the time, I was not clear about why Mother was telling me this story. I thought it was a cautionary tale to keep me from getting too curious and running off the property and getting hurt or lost. I felt concern for this Yvonne cow and wondered why on earth she'd be so silly. But I also thought it was strange for Mother to be telling me something so morbid. It wasn't what you might describe as her style.

"Audrey, there was another famous escape, and this one happened not too far from where we are right now. There were two cows, April and May. They were being transported in a small truck. But as it made its way through the city, the traffic got heavy and everything came to a standstill. These two large ladies managed to push up against one side of the truck until their weight toppled it, and the metal gate broke open. April and May bolted out like rodeo broncos." Oh my, I thought, how exciting! This story had action, maybe danger. "What happened, Mother?" I asked, with much more curiosity. "Well, Audrey, the humans brought in dozens of police. They came with lasso ropes and guns. But the cows were not deterred, dodging among the cars and trucks and bowling over anyone in their way as they searched for a way out. It went on for a very long time, but in the end, they were caught and herded onto another truck and taken on their way." Mother paused and looked out in the distance.

I was still taking in the tribulations of April and May, disappointed with the ending to their adventure and wondering if I preferred the mystery of Yvonne's disappearance instead. I know what Agnes would say.

Mother turned back to look at me. Her voice changed. It was sharper, more determined. I was frightened, as she had never spoken to me like that before. "We are proud animals, Audrey. Don't let anyone tell you differently. We may look docile, and perhaps most of us do accept our lot without complaint, but don't think that we wouldn't rush out into the world beyond the electric fences and find our place in the wild if given half a chance. Do you understand what I'm saying? None of us talk about it, but that's because it's buried deep inside, asleep and often forgotten. Most don't even know it's there." Mother looked at me, and she was both sad and beautiful, and I loved her so much.

"I think I do, Mother," I said. "I think I know that feeling that you're talking about. It's hot and alive, and I feel it just after I wake up in the morning, but before I open my eyes, when I know there's a new day ahead of me, and I don't know what's going to happen. Is that the feeling? Because if that's what you mean, then I think I understand." Mother came over and licked my face. She was smiling again. "I know you do, Audrey. I always did."

MADGE

(cow)

Yes, yes, I've heard those stories, but I remain doubtful. It's all pie-in-the-sky wishing, plain and simple. These legends get passed on from cow to cow, farm to farm. But stories aren't rocks. Rocks don't lose their basic shape, but stories are bendable and twistable, and who knows which cow added a word here or an extra sentence there. Some so desperately want to believe that a cow in the wild can survive forever and not be found that they change the story to feed that desire. But I can't live off false hope. I can't pretend that Lon is—that he might . . . ahem, I'm sorry, but I wasn't built to think that way. Maybe Yvonne of Bavaria did manage to stay free, but in my opinion, she was as likely to have been caught an hour later. Not that I had the heart to tell Audrey such cold truths just after they took her mom away.

AGNES

(cow)

No, I never heard that one. Whoa! That is like so—whoa! Spooky, eh? But what do you mean, *Yvonne just disappeared*? Like "poof, she's gone" gone? Holy human, that's a mystery for sure! I once saw a spaceship fly over the farm, you know.

AUDREY

(cow)

They took Mother away the next afternoon. I knew something was not quite right, but as I said earlier, I would not allow myself to consider what that might be. Mother spent the whole morning in my company, nuzzling and grooming me like I was a newborn. She didn't say much at all, and I, out of nervousness I suppose, talked up a storm. I explained about Eddie's new mooching trick in which he performs a half flip in the air. I filled her in on the rift among the geese over a comment regarding a certain someone's waddle that no apology could overcome. I described Little Girl Elspeth's new Sunday dress with the bright floral print, and how half those flowers looked good enough to eat. Mother laughed at that, and I was relieved. But then the truck pulled onto the property.

A hush settled around the farm. The chickens stopped their complaining, the sheep put an end to their latest debate, and all you could hear was mud sloshing as Buster tried impossibly to hide away in his pen as he always did in those situations. I could feel Mother's heart speed up a notch.

Everything sped up. I was confused and afraid, unsure of what was happening. The latch of the carriage door squealed open. Human steps shuffled closer. Before I even realized it, Mother was up. "Stay here with Madge," she said. I did as I was told.

In hindsight, I realize there were precious seconds before Mother was led from the barn and out of sight. I could have said something. I could have said "I love you, Mother" or "Wait for me" or . . . or "Don't be scared."

The truck drove off, followed by a giant sigh, as if all the animals on the farm had been holding their breath.

MADGE

(cow)

The poor girl stood in the same place for hours after that blasted truck took Jeanine. Heart-wrenching. The child was stunned for several days. She would barely eat, would barely move unless she heard a motor vehicle approaching. Then she'd bolt toward the yard, and you just knew she was expecting to see her mother back from whatever mysterious trip she'd been on. Yes, it was heart-wrenching, plain and . . . (*sigh*) simple.

EDDIE

(dog)

Audrey was sad and lonely. She didn't want to play or go exploring or any of the things we used to have fun doing together. I couldn't do anything to cheer her up either. Dad said to leave her be, but I didn't want to. Jeepers, Audrey was my friend! It hurt me to see her so miserable! I tried bringing some of her favorite flowers from the far hill. I'd drop them by her side, and she'd look at them and say thanks. But the next day they would still be right where I left them.

AUDREY

(cow)

Nothing felt the same after Mother was taken away. My world was topsy-turvy. I could not make sense of life. It had suddenly become unjust and cruel—or indifferent. Yes, indifferent is the word, as indifferent as inclement weather. There were thunderstorms and hailstorms inside me. Thick fog patches filling up my head. Cold, stabbing ice running through my veins, and my heart shriveled up by a relentless drought. I was bereft of my mother's nourishing love.

In fairness, most of the animals were kind to me, and if not kind, then respectful. Farmer even came by with Little Girl Elspeth, who stroked my flank gently and sang a lullaby. I was touched, moved by such attentive gestures, even if I might not have been able to show it at the time. But strangely, it was an act of meanness that finally shook me out of my gloom.

Norma was holding court with some of the ladies, as is her practice, going down her weekly list of animals deserving of ridicule. I was tucked away in a dark corner of the barn, unseen, and I might have paid them no mind, had it not been for hearing my name. "And what about little orphan Audrey?" Norma sniggered. "How many days is that girl going to wear a cloud over her head like a spring bonnet? I assumed that with her over-the-top imagination, she'd be thinking her mother had pulled an Yvonne and ended up in Cow Paradise instead of Abbot's War."

Upon hearing Norma's words, I was overcome by two conflicting emotions, both as powerful as water blasts from the nozzle of the barn's cleaning hose. Up until that moment, I never allowed myself to acknowledge that Mother had been taken to Abbot's War. Mother was absent, yes, but not *gone*; nothing so final as that.

Of course it was obvious, but when you're truly afraid, your mind can play tricks on you. Hearing it from Norma's spiteful mouth finally woke me up. But the mention of Yvonne of Bavaria was like a magic spell. It was as though hearing those words allowed me to suddenly grow wings and fly above Bittersweet Farm and the thick sorrow that surrounded me, so that I could see farther than I ever had before. Maybe Mother did "pull an Yvonne" as Norma put it. Why not? Mother was clever. Why on earth would she

tell me stories of cows who had escaped if she wasn't intending to be one herself?

EDDIE

(dog)

Darn tootin', it was great! It was as if someone had flicked a switch on Audrey! One second she was as silent and still as Corner Rock, and the next she was back to her usual Audrey self . . . well, mostly. Ah, heck, it was still swell because I

had missed her. So it didn't make any difference whether she was going on a mile a minute about the grass-tasting tour of Europe she was planning, or about how her mom escaped and was living the good life. All I knew was that Audrey was back to being her old, terrific self, and I was tail-wagging happy! I remember telling Dad about Audrey's return to good spirits. All he said was, "Best not get too close to a cow of her category."

MADGE

(cow)

I couldn't let it continue. Jeanine had put Audrey's care into my hooves, and I wasn't about to let the girl live in some fantasyland forever. She had to face the facts, plain and simple. Audrey had to come back to earth. She didn't understand yet how the world worked. Those stories about escape were offering nothing but future pain. She was probably thinking Jeanine tipped the truck like April and May, and now she was living in some cow's paradise. Let me be clear here—I wasn't trying to be cruel in order to get Audrey to accept her mother's death. I was more concerned that Audrey should accept that her mother's fate would also be her own.

AUDREY

(cow)

Clover green, a tasty treat
I'm grateful for each one I eat

And there was Madge, giving it to me straight. I panicked. I admit it, I did. The truck will come for me as well? I too am destined for Abbot's War? "You're not a child anymore," Madge said. "You need to know." Not a child. Yes, I understood, but then is that what growing up is all about? Learning one piece of horrible information after another? Is there no joy or hope mixed in there too? How much pain and sorrow was my poor heart to bear? Eddie, bless his big, *big* heart, held onto hope like it was his favorite bone. "Don't worry, Audrey," he said over and over. "We'll figure something out. You bet we will. Darn tootin', I promise." Oh, Eddie, what would I have done without my faithful, loyal friend?

Later, I made my way to Viewing Hill on my own. You can do your best thinking on Viewing Hill. I should have been distraught, but I kept hearing Eddie's voice in my head. "We'll figure something out, Audrey." And I was thinking of Mother telling me the stories of Yvonne of Bavaria, and April and May on the highway. And then I remembered one other thing Mother said to me, something I didn't think was important at the time because Mother often said things like that. It was when we were returning from the grove, and I suppose I was impatient to find Eddie and tell him everything I had just learned. Mother said, "Audrey, I'm not as fast or agile as I used to be. Why don't you run up ahead?" I was hesitant, because I thought it would be rude to leave Mother. But then she laughed and added, "There are lots of pleasures in this world, my dear daughter, but nothing gives me more joy than watching you rushing off, all full of life and free as a bird."

Then it dawned on me. Mother hadn't been telling me what *she* intended to do; she was telling me what *I* should do. Be free. Be free as a bird. Stay alive, Audrey, I could hear her voice saying in my head. Stay alive. Be free. Escape.

THE PLAN

2

AUDREY

(cow)

She, who was dear
She, who gave light
Suddenly gone
I'm left with just night
But days never stop
And still I grow older
One day, I pray
Let me grow bolder

Time flies. It did for me, anyway. In the blink of an eye, a couple of months had passed. But even still, a lot happened. I didn't forget about Mother, whom I continued to miss and think of every single day. And I didn't ever forget what Madge had told me, not for a second.

When I look back at that period, it makes me smile, because I really hadn't understood how the world worked yet. Eddie and I truly thought that the truck could come for me at any moment and that my plan for escape had to happen as soon as possible. I was a desperate cow. We searched the farm's border fences looking for any weaknesses, gaps or loose posts that might give way to a shove. The only one worth trying to knock over ended up giving me a painful sliver, and poor Eddie was required to pull it out with his teeth. It was not pleasant. Eddie was what you might call a jumpy surgeon.

Then I suddenly remembered an important detail from the Yvonne of Bavaria story that I had overlooked. Before slipping into the forest, Yvonne needed to jump over a fence. I relayed this detail to Eddie, suggesting that perhaps I should concentrate on learning how to fling myself over an obstacle, rather than through it or under it. Eddie didn't share my optimism, and I admit that I am not the most athletic of animals, being more graceful with a turn of phrase than a turn of body. However, when you take into account our long friendship and Eddie's gentle soul, I really didn't expect him to fall on his back laughing at my idea for quite so long a time.

EDDIE

(dog)

Aw, I confess, it wasn't very swell of me. But Audrey is a cow, and cows are . . . well, jeepers, cows are big! When she was a calf, Audrey could move a bit, and we would even chase each other for short spurts. But I've never seen one of the adult cows hold a leg up without wondering if they would topple over the next moment. Trying to picture Audrey flying through the air like Middle Boy Lester on his outdoor trampoline was too funny. Audrey doing belly flops and back flips, munching on clover between bounces? No, I shouldn't have behaved the way I did. The situation was serious. Maybe that's why I laughed—to get rid of all the nervousness and fear I had scampering around inside me.

AUDREY

(cow)

Ridiculous or not, I had to try. And truthfully, it wasn't pretty. I wasn't a young calf anymore, and trying to push off with my back legs required more physical effort than I was used to, not to mention my natural lack of coordination.

Seen from Eddie's perspective, I'd probably be laughing too. So, far from any prying eyes, I practiced and practiced for days and eventually could manage a leap over a fallen log. Perhaps leap is too dramatic a word, but I did get over it, and even Eddie was impressed. But we both realized that a log was nothing like a border fence, and I was no closer to escaping Abbot's War with this newly acquired ability.

EDDIE

(dog)

Then I had an inspiration! I said to Audrey, "If jumping over a fence is out of the question, then how about walking over it?" She didn't understand, so I had to demonstrate. See, Middle Boy Lester had been teaching me what he called "circus tricks." Back behind Farmer's house, he would place a wooden plank between two ladders. I would climb up the rungs of one ladder, balance my way across the plank, and go down the other ladder. Gosh, what I'll do for a treat sometimes—it's embarrassing! But anyway, I dragged a plank out into the field to show Audrey what I was thinking. I put one end of it on top of the log that she was learning to jump over, see, to create a sloped walkway. Then I simply made my way up the plank to the top and jumped down the other side. Ta-da!

AUDREY

(cow)

Eddie thought that if we could find a plank big and strong enough to hold my weight, we could lean it against the top of the border fence, and I could do basically that same "trick." Instead of learning to jump higher, I'd need to practice maintaining my poise on an incline, which still wasn't easy, and still required much practice, but in the balance, so to speak, seemed more doable. Oh, how I practiced, practiced and failed, failed and practiced, over and over. And that was not even putting the wood at an angle yet! Just walking across it flat on the ground was challenge enough. Then we tried spanning it over a gap so I'd get over any fear of heights. That was Eddie's concern, which was never my concern until he put that fear into my head, and even now, to this day, I still have a fear of heights.

I don't know if the plan would have worked. Everything felt so urgent, and there were so many uncertainties. How would we get a plank long enough to reach the top of the fence at an angle I could manage? Who would help us lift it? Where would we put it so no one could see? But it was the best plan we had at the time, so I kept at it, trying to stay positive, trying to get better, practicing from sunrise to sundown. And then Eddie's dad changed everything.

MAX

(dog)

Right, you're here about that Audrey story. Fine. One minute, understood? I'll give your question one minute and we're through. Have I made myself clear? (*hmph*) So . . . I put in a solid day's work, and when I'm done, I expect to be done. The last thing I want, once I finish getting the sheep to where they're supposed to be, is to have Farmer tell me to run off to the far end of the farm to fetch a wayward cow. This was going on day after day with Audrey. I wasn't sure why at first, but then I saw Audrey doing stuff that a cow shouldn't be doing, and risking a broken leg by doing it. I could see where it was all heading, and I knew that Farmer would not be pleased. I suspected Eddie might have had something to do with it too, because he and Audrey had been close since birth. (*hmph!*) Children. They can be so darn . . . childish. This girl really hadn't a clue.

When I'd finally had enough of her nonsense, the day that I caught her balancing along some board across an irrigation ditch, I said to her, "You're not fat enough." I remember that she looked at me with her head slightly tilted and replied, "Excuse me?" I repeated myself. "I said that you're not fat enough to worry about being taken to Abbot's War. I know for a fact that every cow that's gone there has been older than you and fatter than you."

I'll give Audrey her due. She didn't waste time pretending that she wasn't up to some sneaky business. She didn't claim that she had no idea what I was talking about, in some la-di-da voice like Norma or Greta would use. No, not her. You could see her brain whirling, taking in the information and figuring out her next move. Without skipping a beat, she asks me, "How much time do you figure I have?" "A year," I said. She nodded. Then she asked, "And weight? How much heavier

would I have to get?" "I'd say two hundred pounds, at least."
And that was that. Okay, we're done.

AUDREY
(cow)

Max's information was invaluable. I felt as if I had been
granted a temporary pardon; as if I had been sentenced to
hang, and at the last moment it was put on hold. I still had
the noose around my neck, but now it was looser, and I could
breathe more easily. I had time on my hooves. Of course, I
couldn't do anything about getting older, but I did have some
say in how much bigger I would get.

EDDIE
(dog)

"Change in plan," she said. "I'm going on a diet." Uh-huh.
You want to run that by me again, Audrey? Once she
explained, I could see her point. It made sense, right? But
jeepers creepers, for a cow that's easier said than done.
Audrey loved to eat. All cows love to eat! But Audrey, she
really enjoyed every bit. Gosh, dieting took a whole lot of

self-control on her part. Sometimes I'd see her hesitate next to a patch of clover. She'd stare at it forever, smelling it and licking it a bit. Hard? Darn tootin' it was hard! You could see the pain in her eyes. This went on for a while. At first no one noticed, but then it must have been brought to Farmer's attention, because suddenly Audrey was being weighed every week, and after that, the vet was called in.

ELSPETH

(human)

I told Daddy. I said, "Audrey isn't feeling good." Daddy saw that I was right . . . but he didn't understand.

DOC
(human)

Yes, I was called down to Bittersweet Farm to check on their Charolais. There was some concern about whether this young cow had a stomach ailment that was preventing her from eating properly and gaining the weight appropriate for her age. I found nothing wrong with her physically; no worms or infections—a bit of a mystery.

ELSPETH
(human)

They didn't understand. Audrey was sad because her mommy was gone away. I would be sad too.

DOC
(human)

Hmm? Well, yes, Glenn did mention that this cow's mother had been sent to the abattoir about four months earlier. There is evidence that animals can suffer from grief upon the loss of a family member. I could only speculate whether that was the case with this particular Charolais.

AUDREY

(cow)

As hard as it was to resist indulging in the sweet, sweet flavors of grass and flower, my plan was working; attention was now drawn to how drawn I looked. To add to my image as a wan and withered cow barely worth the gas money to drive to Abbot's War, I would suck in my four stomachs whenever Farmer was nearby. I daresay I looked haggard and hardly appetizing. My performance was convincing to the point that a certain cow, namely Greta, took it as a challenge to her reputation.

GRETA

(cow)

Who did she think she vas, ya? Vat did she know of life's slings and arrows? Does a bit of skinniness compare to how I have suffered in this cruel vorld? I try to be brave, ya, and strong, ya, not for myself, but for all animals on this farm, yet no vun could see my sacrifice anymore! It hurts to remember such a difficult time.

AUDREY

(cow)

There is such a thing as *too* good a performance, I learned. I was drawing the wrong kind of attention from Farmer. One evening, Roy approached me. He said, "L'il Audrey, you'd best be strappin' on the feedbag. There's been talk around the dinner table that if you don't improve your weight soon, they will be forced to consider drastic measures." I didn't need to ask Roy to clarify what he meant by "drastic measures" because the tone in his voice said it all. Too fat or too skinny, the truck to Abbot's War had my name on it.

So I took Roy's advice. I started to eat with gusto. Not too challenging a task, as you can imagine. And I suppose that the routine of eating, and the pleasure of it, made the worry of being sent to Abbot's War lessen. It's hard to stay anxious about something, day after day, even something horrible, when it's so far away in the future. When the world continues to be filled with splendor? When beauty is splashed across the landscape or detailed on the feathers of a perched flicker? I couldn't help but be lulled into a sense of wonder and joy, for wasn't that what I feared losing in the first place?

Days turned into weeks, and weeks turned into months. Life went on, as they say. It wasn't as if Max's warning had been completely forgotten. The words "fatter" and "older" continued to hover around my head like bothersome mosquitos. I just grew better and better at ignoring them.

Mother was never too far from my heart. I spoke to her in whispers when among others. But when I was alone on Viewing Hill, I talked to her out loud, making note of the changes in season that she herself would have pointed out for my benefit. I cherished those times to be close, even though there was a lump of sorrow stuck in my throat. "Mother," I'd say, "the leaves are turning. See? There are some streaks of yellow and orange on the slopes behind Sky View Farms." I felt extra joy sharing these observations with her. "Snowflakes, Mother! Look, I can catch them on my tongue!" Seasons passed in bliss. And then one day, Roy came by while I was communing with Mother. "It's time," he said.

ROY

(horse)

I heard it at Farmer family's chow-down the evenin' before. Farmer's announcement didn't go well. Little Girl Elspeth done had herself a tantrum and was sent up to her room without dessert. But the decision still stuck. Audrey was going. By rights, I should have talked to Audrey straight-away, as is my custom. But I dilly-dallied because . . . well, because I did not trust that I could keep my emotions close to my chest. By golly, I was the farm newspaper, and I had an obligation to give the news steady and without feeling. If I peppered it with fear and sadness, then how was a young cow like Audrey to accept it? So I waited until the next day. When I saw her up on Viewing Hill all by her lonesome, I figured now would be the opportune moment. "It's time, Audrey," I said. "They've made the arrangements."

Shoot. Never had I felt so guilty about bein' the messenger as I did at that moment. I could see the shock in her sweet face. She fought like a polecat to keep herself from unraveling, forcing herself not to shy away. "When?" she asked. "Three days from now," I told her. "Truck's expected

at noon." Her legs were tremblin', but she held her ground, Audrey did. Her eyes did not break contact with mine, and in the long seconds that passed, I watched them change like the weather, from moist and sorrowful to steely hard like ice on Artificial Lake. "I'm not going gently, Roy," she said. "You hear me?" She had spunk, that Audrey, there was no denying it. I certainly was not going to tell her to do otherwise. I gave her a respectful nod before leaving. "You do what you need to, Miss Audrey. And if help is required, I hope you will not hesitate to call upon old Roy."

EDDIE

(dog)

I was coming back to the barns with Dad and the sheep when we saw Roy heading up Viewing Hill. I already knew that Audrey was there. I'd caught her scent downwind an hour earlier. I always left Audrey alone when she was on Viewing Hill, because that was her private time with her memories of her mom. But jeepers, seeing Roy going up to meet her made my heart skip a beat! We all stopped; sheep and cows, even Dad, yes sirree. Audrey and Roy were squared off, two figures alone on the hill. No one could hear what they were saying, but we all knew just the same. When Roy turned away, I turned to Dad. He gave me a nod and I left him with the sheep, running as fast as my four legs could take me. See, I hadn't forgotten about Abbot's War, and I'd been doing some pretty serious thinking. Aw, heck, I didn't have a plan or nothing. But I did have a plan about getting a plan!

AUDREY

(cow)

I don't know if you have been as fortunate in your life to have as good a friend as I've had in Eddie. Mother said that Eddie and I used to cozy up to each other for afternoon naps soon after I came into the world. Eddie never really had a chance to get to know his mother because he was brought to the farm as a little pup. Mother said Eddie was there when I was born, fascinated with the whole birthing process and wide-eyed in surprise at seeing how tall I was when I finally stood up. Eddie swears he can still remember snuggling up with me against Mother's flank, content in the envelope of warmth but always a bit wary that I might crush him one day. Dear Eddie, how I miss you. What is a good friend? A good friend is one that takes the lead to help you, even when they know that by helping you, they will lose you. That's a good friend. That was Eddie.

EDDIE

(dog)

Gosh, I stood across from Audrey at the exact same spot where Roy had just been. And at first, we didn't say a thing! I swear I had a million yaps inside me wanting to come out, but nothing did; we just stood silent. I don't know why. Maybe 'cause there was too much to say and we didn't know where to start.

AUDREY

(cow)

Maybe it was the knowing that things would never be the same again, that Eddie and I had reached a turning point, chosen not by us but dictated by circumstances out of our control. Suddenly, we seemed older, not children anymore. Just like that. It was what Mother might call a solemn moment. So we gave it the respect it rightly deserved. Those moments are like the dog-eared creases that Middle Boy Lester bends into the top corners of the pages of his favorite books. They are the bookmarks of all the significant bits in the stories of our lives. But when the urgency of the situation demanded our full focus, Eddie said—

EDDIE
(dog)

"We need help, Audrey," is what I said. "Jeepers, we're trying to figure this out on our own, but we're not up for the task. We need someone smarter." Audrey nodded slowly. "Who did you have in mind?"

BUSTER
(pig)

Oh dear, oh dear, oh dear. Well, I like solving puzzles, yes, yes, I do. Been like that all my life. Riddles and math problems, brain teasers, memory games, and uh, yes, yes, pattern recognition. Interesting story, I once came across a partly filled Sudoku puzzle on a piece of newspaper that blew right into my sty! And I, uh, I finished the rest of it in my head, yes, yes, I did. Way too soon, though. I wish I could have made it last longer. My brain is, uh, yes, yes, pretty big, you understand. It needs stimulation and exercise. Agnes comes around, yes, every so often to ask me a question. Things that keep her up at night, like, uh, oh my, well, mainly about space aliens. But other than that, no one is interested in my brain. Oh, no, no, no. No one is much interested in me, period. So I was, uh, quite, yes, quite surprised when Eddie and Audrey dropped by.

EDDIE

(dog)

I don't know why I hadn't thought of it earlier! Buster is the go-to pig for figuring things out. Gosh, he can stare at a bucket of animal feed and tell you what percentage is fish meal, corn kernels, alfalfa pellets or sunflower seeds! Dad told me that when Buster was a piglet, he not only figured out how to get into Farmer's house, but he managed to open their fridge and get at a strawberry pie. And Dad said that was just the time Buster got caught! Jeepers, which means he was probably doing it a whole bunch of times before that. But the thing about Buster is that his confidence isn't so great anymore, so you have to appeal to his self-esteem, otherwise fear can make him freeze up.

AUDREY

(cow)

I forgot how much Eddie got around on the farm, and I really didn't give him credit for the relationships he'd forged with all the animals, four-legged and otherwise. I would not have considered Buster as a source of expertise in the escape department. He always struck me as the nervous type, and a loner, and way more concerned about his next meal than even myself. Which only goes to show that I too have my blind spots.

I followed Eddie to Buster's pen. I kept quiet because it was clear that Eddie had been giving this meeting some thought. So as not to alarm him, Eddie casually said, "Buster, suppose, just for fun, that an animal wanted to escape Bittersweet Farm. Is it possible?" Nevertheless, Buster started hyperventilating on the spot. "W-w-why would an animal do that? Is s-s-something wrong with Farmer? Is he sick? Did he go broke? Are the food deliveries being canceled?" We needed ten full minutes to calm Buster down and reassure him that he'd still get fed. Eddie tried again, "Jeepers, it's just a riddle. Everything's fine.

You're brilliant at riddles, right, Buster? Now, I say it's impossible to escape, but Audrey thinks it can be done. What do you think?"

Buster didn't even pause to consider. "Of course it's possible. Can't go through the fences, though, oh, no, no, no. Farmer checks them every year. Latches are easy to open, yes. The best bet would be to go, uh, yes, to go right through the front entrance. But it would be useless to do that, on account of all the fences separating the farms in the area.

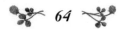

Oh dear, oh dear, oh dear, you're sure to get caught out on the road in no time."

Buster turned toward his food trough to focus on what was left of his slop while Eddie and I shared a look of hopelessness. From what Mother had tried to tell me, I understood that I needed to find a way to reach the forest. Yet how could I reach it if the whole area is sectioned off with one fence after another, preventing me from going anywhere other than the road? It was so discouraging. But after a few mouthfuls, Buster said, "If an animal really wanted to escape for good, they'd have to do it while in transport."

EDDIE

(dog)

Audrey's ears perked up, and darn tootin', I knew why! See, Audrey's mom had told her a story about two cows who tried to get away while being transported on a truck. But the confusing thing was that those cows got caught, so we weren't sure what Buster meant. So Audrey asked him, "Would you agree that the forest is the best place to aim for?" Buster said, "Obviously. It offers camouflage and, uh, yes, yes, lots of hiding places." Then Audrey said, "But it would be too dangerous to jump off a moving truck, and it would be pointless to wait for it to stop, so what do you mean, Buster? How could I—I mean, how could someone get the truck to stop by a forest?"

BUSTER
(pig)

"Flat tire," is what I said, yes, yes, I did. I would have thought that was obvious, but I, uh, no, no, I shouldn't assume that everyone's brain is as big as mine. They still couldn't follow my thinking. I had to walk them through it. I said, "If you puncture a front tire beforehand, you can, uh, yes, yes, you can time the leak so that the tire flattens out right beside a forest. Get me a map, and I can do the calculations."

EDDIE
(dog)

Gosh, I'm thinking two things now. First, jeepers creepers, we just hit the jackpot! And second, where in the world are we going to get ourselves a map? But Buster is looking up at the position of the sun and telling me that there should be a map by the phone in Farmer's kitchen and that it can be accessed through the open window over the sink. And if I go in exactly fifteen minutes, the Farmer children will still be in school, Farmer lady will be in the office doing the accounting, and Farmer will just be heading to the milking station.

AUDREY

(cow)

Buster turned out to be a master strategist. At the designated time, Eddie jumped through the kitchen window and retrieved the map unseen, just as Buster predicted. Eddie rushed back to the pen and unfolded the map, and we both watched Buster study it carefully. Finally, he stuck his snout on a spot on a line next to a big patch of green. "Here," he said. "That would be the best place to stop a truck if it was heading to Abbot's War." Those last two words took my breath away. Eddie didn't catch on, but I was fully aware that we had never once mentioned Abbot's

War when we posed our escape riddle to Buster. I didn't say anything, though. Meanwhile, Buster is making all these calculations in his head involving the pound per square inch pressure of a truck tire, the average speed a truck would be going, and the required size of hole needed to release enough air to cause a flat tire and make the driver stop on the road beside the forest. As Eddie would say, gosh! and jeepers creepers!

BUSTER

(pig)

You don't want to use a nail, no, no, no, because the air will go out too quickly. A screw is best for a delayed leak. Interesting fact: I have a collection of items I keep hidden away in the corner of my sty, yes, yes, I do. You never know when a piece of metal might come in handy.

EDDIE

(dog)

He had pocketknives, bottle caps, saw blades, a flashlight, two license plates and even a tube of lipstick! From among all that, Buster roots out a six-inch screw and says that will do the job. Then it suddenly dawned on me—he was treating this pretend riddle as the real situation that it was. Which meant one of two things: he was either too caught up in the exercise to stop, or he knew what we were up to and was making himself an accomplice. In any case, we still had a problem. The screw needed to be mounted on a thin piece of wood so it could stand straight up, with the pointy part in the air. That's where being a human with arms, hands and thumbs has its advantages. Fortunately, Audrey came up with a solution.

ROY

(horse)

Heh, heh, heh. Oh, I reckon a carpenter would have approached the design with more grace, and certainly by using a screwdriver as well. But I appreciate that Miss Audrey came to me for assistance. Nothin' like the strong *clomp* of a horseshoe to drive a screw through a piece of pine. I didn't ask questions, by golly, even though only a few hours earlier, I'd spotted Eddie leaping in and out of the same window where I do my best carrot-mooching. But my interest was most definitely piqued.

AUDREY

(cow)

One winter, I watched Middle Boy Lester make a ball of snow at the top of Viewing Hill. Once it reached the size of a curled-up lamb, he pushed it over the side. That ball of snow grew larger and larger as it picked up speed. That's the

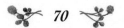

best way I can explain how it felt to be caught up in Buster's planning—things kept getting bigger and moving faster.

BUSTER

(pig)

Well, time was a factor, and, oh dear, oh dear, oh dear, there were still a lot more details to make this plan work. For example, I had to teach Audrey how to open a slide latch from the inside of the truck, yes, yes, I did. I have a similar one on my pen. When I was not so big as I am now, and not so nervous, no, no, no, I would take this twisty hook, which has a little doughnut hole lasso, that I could use to snag the bulb at the end of the bolt. Then I'd, yes, yes, pull it upward to get the bolt free so that I could take it out of the latch and then open the gate. Twelve seconds is my all-time best record.

AUDREY

(cow)

Easier said than done, I'm afraid. Besides which, I had to learn how to keep that little contraption hidden in my mouth without swallowing it. So with only two days left until the truck arrived, whenever Farmer family was out of sight, I'd sneak into Buster's pen and practice. Buster would motivate me with the egg timer he had borrowed from Farmer's kitchen many years ago. Eventually I could do it, although not nearly as fast as General Buster would have preferred. I could only hope that the latch on the Abbot's War truck would be no more difficult than the one I was already struggling with. Meanwhile, Eddie had to work on all the other parts of Buster's plan.

EDDIE

(dog)

Buster pointed out that the tire had to be punctured with the screw while the truck was in the farmyard. First we'd have to place the screw under the tire. Then, up in the cab, the gear needed to be shifted into neutral so we could roll the truck on top of the screw. "Jeepers!" I cried. "Pushing a truck is no easy business. Why the heck can't we just let the driver drive the truck over the screw?" Pretty good thinking on my part, if I do say so myself. Buster simply sighed and rolled his little eyes and then explained that when the truck left Bittersweet Farm, the driver backed up fifty-two percent of the time, and drove forward forty-eight percent. . . . Gosh, some of the stuff Buster keeps in his head is a bit weird.

In any case, the odds were too close to take a chance on putting the screw in front of the tire or behind, so pushing the truck ourselves was the only option. Obviously we couldn't do that right under Farmer's nose. Therefore a distraction would be required to keep all the humans busy while we performed the operation. What kind of distraction? One that I could scramble up in less than thirty-six hours!

CLARK

(sheep)

Before we answer your question, let me be clear: we are a terribly misjudged group. What has been understood as random movement in which one of us changes position and the rest then follow brainlessly is untrue. Take the time to listen to our passionate bleats and you will see that a shift from one location to another has everything to do with the force of the argument being brought by a member of the flock. Sheep speak eloquently and are very convincing. If we all follow a ram one way, and then follow a ewe somewhere else, you can be sure it's because we weighed the arguments and came to a hard-earned decision. There are much more weak-minded things to be in the world than a herd of sheep.

LIONEL

(sheep)

Well said, Clark, well said. Ahem . . . the request was brought forward during one of our evening scrums. That is when the herd votes on the issues that need attention before we all retire for the night. We sleep on the decisions and then re-vote in the morning.

BRIGIT

(sheep)

Unless, of course, a member wakes up and demands a debate prior to sunrise. Then, according to Rule 463-B of the Sheep

Constitution, the herd is required to get up and hash out the concerns of that member to her or his satisfaction.

LIONEL

(sheep)

Yes, good point, Brigit. Now, on the night in question, Eddie interrupted our meeting. He requested that we create a distraction at a certain place and time. This brought up an issue right away. We sheep are not in the habit of including any

other animal, especially a sheep-*dog*, in our meeting. Max and his son, Eddie, are tolerated but not embraced. They are what we consider necessary evils.

BRIGIT
(sheep)

What Lionel means is that we acknowledge that the sheep-*dog* does protect us from dangerous predators like wolves, foxes, etcetera, for which we are grateful. But we also point out that the sheep-*dog*'s duty is primarily to Farmer, and the rights of us sheep come second. Ultimately, the dog orders where we sheep are to go and how long we are allowed to stay there. Until sheep are granted full power to decide where on the farm we will graze, our sheep dignity is being denied, and we will be forever at odds with dogs such as Max and Eddie.

LIONEL
(sheep)

Hear, hear, Brigit, well put. However, when Eddie approached us with his request, he was speaking on behalf of Audrey, which made the issue, well, less an issue.

BRIGIT

(sheep)

Let it be known that we sheep wholeheartedly recognized and sympathized with Audrey's plight as a food cow. If we hesitated in helping our sister in her time of need, it was because she did not seek us out first, but instead looked elsewhere.

EDDIE

(dog)

Uh . . . no, the sheep weren't our first choice. I figured that being, as they say, a sheep-*dog*, maybe . . . you know, maybe they wouldn't take me seriously, asking them for something. They don't really like my dad. They're probably not thrilled with me either. But that's not the only reason. You've heard how sheep talk, right? As a group, it takes sheep forever to make up their minds about anything. They just talk and talk and talk, and we really didn't have that kind of time to spare. We only had a day and a half left! So first we went somewhere else for help.

LORETTA

(goose)

Who's asking? I'm just saying, who wants to know? Why do *I* want to know who wants to know? Listen, Bub, and you listen good. Loretta is not in the habit of blabbing her beak off to any stranger who comes snooping around with a load of questions. You got that? Loretta would prefer to know the purpose for this line of inquiry before she decides to cooperate. Am I getting through to you? Do I look like some pushover? Is there a sign hung on my tail feathers that reads "CHUMP"? No, there isn't, is there? So let me repeat the follow-up question to the question asked of me: What is this all about, huh? . . . Oh, it's about Audrey. Well, why didn't you say so in the first place! Yeah, we did business with her.

CYD

(goose)

Oh, my. Tsk, tsk, tsk. Dear interviewer, please do not be put off by Loretta. Her speech might be a tad crude, but her heart is golden, I assure you. Yes, it is true that a certain business meeting was conducted between the goose family and one Audrey the cow and one Eddie the dog. Let us not be coy here. We are all adults, are we not, and all of us are aware of the situation pertaining to Audrey, her predicament and her plan to remedy it. She needed a distraction to take place close to the Abbot's War truck. We listened to her request, which is not a crime as far as I know. And let the record show that they approached us and not vice versa. We were minding our own business. As I recall, at the time, Loretta and I were discussing whether to take a stroll toward Artificial Lake.

LORETTA

(goose)

Yeah, right. As I recall, we were discussing the fact that Cyd waddles like she's wearing Little Girl Elspeth's old baby diapers. Ha!

CYD

(goose)

Pardon-moi? Loretta said *what* about me? She did? She mentioned the diaper comment? Really? Oh, my, I . . . I . . .

I so wish that dear Loretta could hold her tongue. What I mean is, I would so, so appreciate it if my oldest and dearest friend could just shut her fat, blabby bill for one merciful second. Do you think that might be possible? Hmm? Do you think that maybe, perhaps, that annoying fowl might shut her stupid, ugly bill?

LORETTA

(goose)

Cyd said *that*? Sounds like someone's got her diapers twisted in a knot. Ha!

CYD

(goose)

Aghhh! You tell Loretta that I will wring her neck! You tell her that if it's the last thing I do, with my dying breath, I will wring her scrawny, stupid neck!

EDDIE

(dog)

So, no, that didn't work out. And that's when I decided we should try the sheep instead. They discussed it all evening, and then they slept on it, and then they woke up and discussed it some more. And then they agreed to do it. And then they didn't. But then they absolutely agreed, and then they discussed *how* they would do it, which took another couple of hours, and jeepers creepers, I think I would rather bite off my own tail than go through that again! We were down to less than a day, but in the end, the sheep settled on a distraction that involved a move rarely done. Gosh, they wouldn't even tell me what it was. So . . .

AUDREY

(cow)

It was done. Eddie had managed to organize all the elements of Buster's plan. Now we just had to wait until noon of the next day to put it all in motion. The quiet before the storm, as they say. Mother's spirit seemed to hover beside me, guiding my heart to a slow, steady rhythm and my mind to an inner peace.

EDDIE

(dog)

I could finally catch my breath. And that's when it really hit me that no matter whether the plan worked and Audrey escaped, or the plan failed and Audrey . . . didn't escape, the one thing that would be the same either way was that I'd never see her again. Just understanding that made me hurt so much inside. I couldn't imagine a day when I wouldn't see Audrey or catch a scent of her on the wind. That last night, I went over to the barn and we lay together for a while. Heck, I'd be lying if I said I didn't whimper. I was losing her. Even if it was for the best, it didn't make the hurt any less painful.

When I headed over to Farmer's house, Dad was waiting for me. "You're breaking all the rules," he said. "Everyone has their place; everyone plays their part. What you're doing is going against the natural order." I looked over at Dad, but I didn't say anything.

AUDREY

(cow)

Gossip spreads through Bittersweet Farm like brush fire. It's a small community. I suppose that within a few hours, everyone other than Farmer family knew that something was up. In the cowshed, it was quiet that evening. Eddie came and stayed a while. We didn't speak. I just gave him some licks around the ears; that's what calms him when he's upset. In my heart, I was sending him all my good wishes, trying not to dwell on our separation.

After he left, I made the rounds of all the ladies. I said good-bye to each of them and wished them nothing but happiness in their lives. I meant it. They were my family, after all. Greta started wailing with big, inconsolable sobs. Agnes became confused and asked if she could just stick to saying good night like she usually did at bedtime. Norma couldn't look me in the eye, but I did hear a quiet "good-bye, child" just as she turned away.

The hardest was saying farewell to Madge. I think for her it brought up memories of her son, Lon. "Mother always felt closest to you," I told her. "She said you were like a walnut fresh off the tree." That got Madge's attention. "Why would she say something like that, Audrey?" she asked. I explained, "Mother said you were hard on the outside, but inside, you were soft and sweet." Madge's eyes got all watery and she came close. "I so want to help you, child, but I can't. I couldn't help my boy either." I was touched that in that moment Madge put me on the same level as her son and that maybe she saw me as a daughter. "It's okay," I said. "Just wish me luck."

THE UNFOLDING

3

AUDREY

(cow)

Nothing new beneath the sun
You've seen it all or so you say
But then a special moment comes
That blithely takes your breath away

Hmm? The inspiration for that poem? I think Norma is the
one you probably should ask.

NORMA

(cow)

Oh, for heaven's sake! *Must* we talk about it? I'd rather not.
I did what I did, and if I knew I'd be scrutinized about it later,
I'd quite certainly not have done it . . . well, maybe not.

AUDREY

(cow)

How is it that horrible things happen on beautiful, sunny
days? Wouldn't it be more appropriate, if you're going to be

miserable or frightened, that it be on a terrible day: a gloomy, gray, wet and cold day? That would then allow the good days to remain untainted, so they can be enjoyed to their full potential.

The day of my escape was probably one of the nicest days that we'd had on Bittersweet Farm that year. The sky was completely clear but for one single cloud, and the breeze being so weak, the cloud stayed in place as if it were pinned there. Mother and I used to interpret cloud shapes when I was little. My imagination was feeble compared to hers, but Mother could always spin my ideas into colorful stories. "Audrey," she'd say, "look at that small, fluffy one. What does it remind you of?" I could have said a half dozen interesting things. I could have said it looked like Middle Boy Lester's toy sailboat that he floats on Artificial Lake, or the humongous mustache on Old Man Farmer who comes visiting from Sky View Farms. But instead, I'd proclaim the most boring and obvious. "It looks like a sheep."

Mother would take it in stride. "Well, yes, Audrey, it is a sheep. That's what happens sometimes to sheep if they get too happy. The happiness fills them up like a balloon

and makes them lighter than air. The next thing you know, the sheep is lifting off the ground and floating away. Farmer must always take the precaution of tying a string around a happy sheep's leg, so that if it starts to rise, he can grab that string and attach it to a fence post. Some days there are so many happy sheep up in the air that you'd think Farmer family was celebrating a birthday." I would have taken her tales as true facts if I hadn't learned to spot the twinkle in Mother's eye. Then we'd share the joke, although I couldn't look at a sheep the same way for quite some time afterward.

By the time of my escape, my imagination had improved, but today it was colored by fear. What I saw in that single cloud against the powder-blue sky reminded me of an angry wolf with its mouth wide open and sharp teeth ready to snap. Hardly what you would call a good omen.

EDDIE

(dog)

None of us met that final morning. See, we figured it might raise suspicion. We all went about our business like it was a regular day. Only when Roy gave the signal would we put the plan into action.

ROY

(horse)

High noon was when we were to get the show started. I stood in a clearing beyond the orchard, watching my long shadow get smaller and smaller as the morning progressed and the sun rose higher. When finally there was nothin' more than a pony attached to my hooves, I moseyed over to the entrance gate all casual-like, pretending to graze but really there to anticipate the truck's arrival. By golly, it was not long before I heard the grunt and growl of its engine. Then it reared its ugly, scarlet head as it climbed up the steep grade about a hundred yards yonder. I turned and made the rounds of notification; first past Audrey in the cowshed, then Buster, then finally the sheep and young Eddie.

KASEY

(human)

Okay, okay, I'll tell you what I saw. But jumpin' June bugs, I've been getting nothing but grief for this since it happened. I'm an independent businessman—hardworking, don't you know—and my reputation is everything. I'd had the delivery contract for the Daisy Dream Abattoir for nearly a decade. I covered all the farms in the Maple Valley—all of them. And there's a lot! My Red Bessie isn't the biggest truck by any stretch, and she isn't new or fancy by an even longer stretch, but she's well-maintained and has been reliable, just as I have been too.

I pulled into Bittersweet Farm at noon, as scheduled. Nothing looked out of the ordinary; everything A-okay. I just had the one pickup, a Charolais. Now, they are one of your bigger cows, so I deliberately didn't book any other pickups for the afternoon. I can fit two regular-sized cows in the carriage comfortably, but if it's a tight fit, it can stress them out. And the Daisy Dream Abattoir owners want a calm cow upon arrival. I can tell you now, though, that once I saw this particular Charolais, I realized that I could probably have fit another one on the truck without any problem and made myself a little extra coin, don't you know. Then again, I might have ended up with two embarrassments instead of one, so I'll just count my blessings.

BUSTER
(pig)

The truck pulled onto the farm and, uh, yes, yes, it turned so that the back was facing the cowshed. Farmer was alone that day. He came over to greet the driver. I saw them shake hands, yes, and then the driver swung open the truck's back gate. It made a terrible squeal. Oh dear, oh dear, oh dear, I don't like that sound. I hide when I hear it. But, uh, no, no, no, not this time! I stood tall, yes, yes, I did. I told Eddie to signal the sheep to get ready to move.

EDDIE
(dog)

Farmer and the driver were heading toward the cowshed, so I ran over to the sheep as soon as Farmer's back was turned. Something didn't feel right. There was a lot of chatter among the sheep, a lot of grumbling mainly. But jeepers, I had no time to ask. I told Clark to get everyone to move into position beside the cowshed door as soon as possible, and then I rushed back to Buster's pen where we had hidden the screw mounted in wood. I grabbed it in my mouth and headed over to the truck. I was supposed to stand it upright, just in front of the tire on the passenger side of the cab. The driver wouldn't likely pay attention to that corner of the vehicle before he drove off. The screw point had to be positioned under one of the grooves in the tire so it could go in deep. Buster knew that the back axle had two tires on each side, so flattening one wouldn't draw much attention. The front axle has just a single tire on each side, which means the driver would be forced to stop to fix a flat. But after I set the screw in place and backed up from under the cab, there was Dad waiting for me, and not looking happy, no sirree.

AUDREY

(cow)

Being stuck in the cowshed, I knew nothing of what was happening near the truck. I heard Farmer and the driver,

though. I heard the scrape of boot soles along the gravel and their conversation getting louder as they approached the spot where I awaited my fate. I was put off by their dull subject matter: talk about gas prices rising and grain prices falling and whether they'll finally put a traffic light at some intersection. Here I was, about to be taken to Abbot's War, in theory, anyway. The least they could do would be to talk about the beautiful weather we were having or the musicality of the word *amaryllis*—talk about something meaningful or say nothing at all and allow my departure to be handled solemnly. In any case, I quickly stuck Buster's twisty thingamajig in my mouth, thus making me the solemn one. Hiding that metal piece rendered me as silent as a centipede that accidentally walked into a rooster meeting.

CLARK

(sheep)

Ahem. Most everyone is acquainted with our group loitering technique, I assume? Briefly, that is when we stand around in a tight bunch, remaining stationary and dense for as long as possible. There's little call for it here on Bittersweet Farm, but it plays well if sheep are being herded along a road and a car comes by. We gather in the middle of the road, blocking traffic and showing what can be achieved by our collective will. Drivers will not test our resolve, and it isn't until the sheep-*dog* is set upon us that we are forced to disperse. However, there is another tactic we can use in nonviolent protest. We call it "the white tornado," although it has also been referred to as "the sheep cyclone" by some. It is a highly advanced move that requires speed, agility and, above all, cooperation. It's extremely difficult to do, and nearly impossible to stop, so is used very sparingly. Once we agreed to get involved, we all voted, after long debate, mind you, to use "the white tornado" as our method of distraction in the Audrey rescue plan, which we code-named Operation Urgent Fury or OUF.

BUSTER

(pig)

I could see Max—Eddie's father—heading toward the truck while Eddie was still underneath it, yes, yes, putting the screw in place. Oh dear, oh dear, oh dear, I should have taken all the variables into consideration: the stuff that, uh, no, no, you can't control or predict, like behavior by other animals. Max was angry. He barked at Eddie, "Just what on earth do you think you're doing, son?" I thought that Eddie might crumble, getting yelled at by his dad, and the plan would be ruined, oh dear. Before I realized what I was doing, I opened the gate to my pen and rushed over. Eddie wasn't backing down though, oh, no, no, no. He, uh, he stood up to Max. He said, "I'm doing what I have to do. I'm doing what needs to be done." Eddie had never spoken to his father like that before. I think it surprised Max, put him back on his heels. Max wasn't yelling now so much as pleading. He said, "We have a job here, son. We work for Farmer. You have to put your feelings aside."

EDDIE

(dog)

I told Dad that I couldn't, not when it concerned Audrey! Gosh, I could have said a lot more too. I could have told him about friendship and love and . . . and doing what's right, yes sirree. But I didn't, because . . . well, jeepers creepers, why should someone have to explain those things? They just are. They're inside all of us, and if someone can't feel them, then how the heck can you even start to make them understand?

BUSTER
(pig)

Now Eddie was supposed to jump in through the window on the driver's side, so he could, uh, yes, yes, put the gearshift into neutral. That way, the truck would be free to move when we pushed it, and we could get the tire on top of the screw. But if, uh, if Eddie moved away from the tire, then Max could have at it. Max said, "I won't let this continue any further." He was just about to dive under the truck, but before he knew it—before *I* knew it—I was there blocking his way, yes, yes, I was! Can you believe it? I was standing up to Max too! I was awesome.

EDDIE
(dog)

Out of nowhere, Buster appears, all three hundred pounds of him! He nudges Dad to the side and plants himself in

front of the truck wheel like a giant pink boulder. Dad's not sure what to do. Does he try to slip around Buster or chew his way through him? I couldn't hang around to find out. I had to trust that Buster could handle it. So I snuck around to the other side and signaled for . . . (*sigh*) my "assistant" to follow me into the cab.

BUSTER

(pig)

Why did Eddie need an assistant? Well, because in order to move the gearshift, you, uh, yes, yes, you have to perform

two operations at the same time. It's easy for humans, but not so easy for us. Who did he have to help him? . . . Um . . . do you *really* need to know?

CHARLTON

(rooster)

I would be delighted to enlighten you in regards to the heroics that I, Charlton the Third, did humbly perform on that illustrious day. You see, when I heard the desperate whispers riding the breeze concerning the escape by one poor, forlorn cow . . . whose name presently eludes me . . . well, I naturally did not wait on ceremony for the concerned parties to come and beg my assistance. Why, that would be unconscionable. I thrust myself in front of those ragtag desperados and declared, "Charlton the Third is at your service!" I daresay they were speechless, and that was quite understandable. Had I been in their hooves and paws, I would have been stupefied and in awe of what stood before me too.

You see, I was a game changer. A *deus ex machina* as the Romans would call it. The odds for success had spiked from zero—no chance—to ninety-nine point nine percent yes chance. That was allowing for a one-tenth percent failure rate, on the remote possibility that I should be struck down by a wayward meteor and rendered unable to complete my mission. How fortunate that cow . . . Amy, was it? . . . how fortunate she was that I was there in the nick of time to save . . . Mandy? No matter, to save that poor cow's life. It's all true. As enthusiastic-but-grossly-unqualified Eddie even said himself, "Charlton, we need you in the clutch!"

EDDIE
(dog)

No, what I said to Charlton was that I needed him *on* the clutch. Jeepers! A clutch is a pedal that humans press down with their foot while changing gears. And the only reason I asked Charlton was because he caught wind of our plans early on, and he's such a bigmouth we were worried that he might spill the beans to Dad, or start crowing at the wrong time during the escape and draw Farmer's attention. I used him where it seemed least likely for him to mess things up. And he was fine, at first, managing to flap up and join me in the cab. Meanwhile, I see Roy heading toward the back of the truck. I tell Charlton to stomp down hard on the clutch while I bite down on the gearshift, ready to move it. But Charlton isn't doing the one simple thing he's supposed to do! Jeepers creepers! Instead, he starts shouting out some crazy speech!

CHARLTON

(rooster)

Why yes, indeed I do remember every word of my soliloquy. I said, "They will talk of this day for years to come! Our names passed down from generation to generation! If we, who go bravely into war, should die upon the battlefield,

let our actions not be in vain. Carry the torch ever onward! For General Buster! For much-too-young Eddie! For valiant and noble and handsome Charlton! And let us not forget our dear, dear sister. Let us not forget dear, dear . . . uh . . . is it Daphne?"

EDDIE
(dog)

"Jump on the clutch!" I barked. I can hear Farmer and the driver coming out of the cowshed with Audrey. "Charlton, jump on the clutch—now!"

KASEY

(human)

Hey, you can believe me or not; I don't care. I saw it all with my own eyes. Me and Glenn Parker are walking the Charolais out of the cowshed. The cow is calm and quiet; it's all as easy as pie. But as soon as we're in the driveway, there's an animal convention happening around my truck!

Jumpin' June bugs, there's a big, angry dog and a fat pig at the far end. They're squared off, and the dog is growling and barking, and it looks as if they're both about to have at it. Meanwhile, there's another dog and a rooster in my cab, don't you know! That dog is barking angry like the first one, and the rooster is crowing like dawn just broke. Then, I see a big old horse at the back end, standing where we're supposed to load the cow. He's staring at us, all friendly at first—I could have sworn he was smiling—but out of the blue, he starts pushing up against the truck with all his strength. And the truck starts rolling forward.

So I leave the cow and rush over to stop the crazy horse and get rid of all these other animals. But suddenly, we're getting swarmed by sheep. I am not making this up! There's three dozen at least! And I'm not talking about a bunch of them standing in our path. No, I'm talking about a whirlwind of sheep circling around us at the speed of sound, like some crazy country fair ride—just a blur of bleats and spinning wool. We were pinned in place. I'd never seen anything like it, well, until my nephew showed me a YouTube clip a week later of something similar, from somewhere up in England. But at

the time, it had us spooked. And then, as if nothing had happened, the sheep stopped. Just like that, they stopped and all started yakking at once.

BRIGIT
(sheep)

It would be inaccurate to say that it happened all at once. Even before Operation Urgent Fury began, certain members of the herd had concerns about the plan.

LIONEL
(sheep)

Brigit is quite correct. It wasn't about the use of "the white tornado," which, for the record, all the sheep wholeheartedly endorsed. No, the disagreement was about whether we should spin in a clockwise direction or counterclockwise. Some might argue that such a detail is pointless, and to that, I can only repeat what I said at the time: "We stand on principle, and we spin on principle too."

BRIGIT

(sheep)

Yes, well put, Lionel, well put. To spin clockwise or to spin counterclockwise, which direction would make the strongest statement? It was an issue that we obviously hadn't debated long enough, so we stopped mid-operation to work it out.

AUDREY

(cow)

There was so much to take in all at once. Obviously the plan wasn't going nearly as well as it should. I couldn't understand what Buster was doing there, not only out of his pen, but standing snout to snout with Max. I could hear Charlton screaming out some speech as if he were rousing the animals to grab pitchforks and attack. But what was most distressing was that the sheep had suddenly stopped their distraction. We all knew that without those few extra seconds, my escape plan was doomed to fail, and my ride to Abbot's War was all but a sure thing. And then . . .

BUSTER

(pig)

And, oh dear, then . . .

EDDIE

(dog)

Gosh, and then . . .

KASEY

(human)

And then (*sigh*), I know you won't believe me. Glenn Parker says I'm exaggerating, but that's just because he's in denial. I saw what I saw, don't you know, and he sure did see it too! So then . . . this cow . . . comes dancing out of the cowshed. You heard me. I mean she was d-a-n-c-i-n-g—DANCING! Sashaying her hips side to side, spinning in little circles, doing little tippy-toe steps, and mooing like she was at the Tuesday karaoke night at Connie's Good Times Grill. Jumpin' June bugs, me and Glenn just stopped in our tracks. My jaw was hanging down so low you could have used my mouth as a breadbox. And I'm thinking, what in the world is going on at Bittersweet Farm?

BUSTER
(pig)

You probably want to know which cow it was. I'd tell you, but, uh, well, she scares me. Yes, yes, she does.

NORMA

(cow)

As I said earlier, I'd rather not discuss it. Simply stated, I could see from where I stood inside the cowshed that the sheep were in disarray, and Farmer was making a beeline to the truck. A distraction was required, so I did the first thing that came to mind. That's all there was to it. Let's move on, shall we?

AUDREY

(cow)

Norma was my guardian angel that day. Mother would have been smiling and laughing, not only at the beautiful spectacle of a cow performing modern dance, but also for the fact that of all the cows, it was Norma who came to my rescue. Norma looked radiant, and she was so brave, knowing that the rest of the ladies would never see her in quite the same light again. I was just as caught up in the distraction as Farmer and the driver, so by the time I was finally led toward the truck, Buster was already slinking back to his pen with the bits of wood that had held the screw. Roy gave a whinny and shook his mane while backing away from the scene. Eddie was on the ground now, with Charlton. He looked my way. When our eyes met, he gave me a nod. Mission completed.

EDDIE

(dog)

Farmer was flustered. He yelled at Dad to get the sheep back to their pen. I joined in to help because I owed Dad that much, although I knew it would still be a while before he'd let me off the hook. But I kept Audrey in sight out of the corner of my eye. I saw the driver slide out a long metal slat from the truck's back and drop the end on the ground with a thud. Then Audrey was led up the ramp in the same way as I had once imagined she might climb to the top of one of the fences and jump to freedom. The driver swung the metal gate shut. Then he slid the latch bolt to lock it in place. While Farmer pushed the ramp back into its sheath, the driver got a clipboard with some paperwork for him to sign.

All that time, Audrey stood up there so still at the back of the truck, with the noon sun lighting her so that she glowed a dazzling white. She looked like a statue, a beautiful statue. It was quiet on the farm, just as it always is during these Abbot's

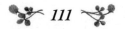

War departures. The sheep didn't make a fuss. They all went along without complaint. Then the driver got in the cab and started up the motor. Suddenly Audrey shifted, turning herself around so that she faced the back, faced us. All the cows began lowing a sad good-bye, Buster joined in with snorts and sobs, and Roy whinnied and raised himself high on his back legs over and over. Even Charlton started crowing. And as the truck began to pull away, away from Bittersweet Farm, away from me, I found it near impossible to let Audrey go, as if there was a cord connected from her heart to mine.

AUDREY

(cow)

Eddie chased after the truck for a while, keeping pace through the gates and down the road. We held our gaze the whole time, squeezing every last drop from the fruit of our sweet friendship. And then, second by second, Eddie began to slow, and he grew smaller and smaller until he was nothing but a dot on the horizon, and I was completely alone.

I watched the gray ribbon of highway spill out from under the truck as if a big spool of it was unraveling behind

us. The road was hilly, climbing high, rolling down into dells, and then cresting yet again, over and over. I was reminded of Middle Boy Lester playing with his toy boat at Artificial Lake, tossing it up and down, talking about storms and crashing waves and calls for rescue. I felt like I was in a storm too, thrown about in a gale, trying to keep balance, trying to stay afloat and not give up hope.

As I grew accustomed to the shifts and concentrated on putting weight to one side and then the other, the shock started to wear off, and I began to take in the surroundings. For the first time in my life, I was off of Bittersweet Farm, the only place I had ever known. I had heard that there were other farms, and I could see Sky View Farms from Viewing Hill, but I had no idea just how many there were. Three Oak Farm, DeLancy Farm, Copper Hill Farm. I passed farms with fancy signs and big metal gates, and simple farms with nothing but a small hand-painted sign next to a gravel road entrance. There were silos and pointy spires sprouting up in the distance in every direction. I saw a giant metal snake running alongside us for a while; its head was roaring louder than Farmer's tractor, and there were clanging bells and flashing lights announcing its arrival at every road crossing. I heard the roar of children rushing about in a play yard, and then more loud clanging bells telling them to stop. I smelled alfalfa and fresh cut grass and blueberry. It was intoxicating. My fear had transformed into excitement.

I confess that for a moment I wished that the truck would never stop. But that foolish thought jarred me into remembering that of course I wanted the trip to end—the whole point was for the trip to end, preferably how and where it was supposed to, with a flat tire next to the large forest. I turned my focus inward again, trying to sense anything different, trying to notice if the truck was leaning or acting up. At first I could find no change whatsoever, but as we continued on, the bumps in the road began to be felt harder from the front end of the truck. It continued to get worse and worse, and it occurred to me that I hadn't seen a farm for quite a long while. All I saw was forest on both sides.

KASEY

(human)

That day was cursed, I tell you, cursed. As if the animals at Bittersweet Farm acting all screwy wasn't enough, my

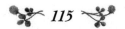

dependable Red Bessie went on the fritz too! As I'm driving along, I'm feeling the occasional *clunk* and then a louder *clunk* and then finally it's all *clunk-dilly-clunk-dilly-clunk-clunk-clunk*. A flat tire! And of course it couldn't be at the back. No, it had to be the front. And of course it couldn't be near one of the gas stations we went past. No, it had to be in the middle of the longest patch of forest on the whole darn trip!

So I pull over to the side and take a look at the problem. Just my luck, I drove over some screw. It's big, and it's wedged in one of the grooves real tight. I mean, it couldn't have been more perfectly placed if it had been done on purpose! Now, I'm working against the clock here. Sure, the cow is calm and docile at the moment, but as the day goes on, she may get cranky, and that's a half ton of cranky, a thousand pounds, so I've got to deal with the situation. But I don't know how! I can't fix the flat with her on the truck adding all that weight. But there's no way I'm going to take her off because I don't have any assistance to make sure I'll be able to get her to go back in afterward.

AUDREY

(cow)

After we came to a stop, I listened as the driver came out to inspect the problem. Then I heard him cursing up a storm, stomping about and kicking the truck, followed by some hobbling and even more cursing. I didn't waste any time. I slid Buster's latch-catcher out of my mouth and kept the end grasped tightly with my teeth. I slipped the noose-end between the slats of the carriage wall and carefully maneuvered it down toward the locking bit on the bolt. I fiddled and fiddled until finally I snagged it.

Suddenly, the driver is walking to the back of the truck, and he's getting himself more and more worked up. I quickly slurped the latch-catcher back into my mouth while he's shouting, "What am I supposed to do now, cow? Hmm? You got a plan? Because I sure don't have a plan!" This was what Mother called a rhetorical question because it didn't require an answer. Humans often talk to us four-leggers without any expectation of a reply.

I remained still and calm, and hoped he didn't notice the bolt's locking bit out of the groove. Lucky for me, he sees a car approaching, so he attempts to flag it down so he can ask them to send a tow truck from the last garage we passed. I go back to my work, catching the locking bit and using it to slide the bolt sideways and out of the latch. As I'm performing this delicate operation, I can hear two voices above me. One of them says, "Check it out! That is so awesome. The cow has got some moves." The other voice is saying, "Totally," over and over.

Once I've finished opening the latch, I look up to discover that the commentators are two crows sitting on a telephone wire. Judging by their vocabulary, I took them to be teenagers. But there was no time for pleasantries. Making sure that the driver was still out of sight and talking to the driver of the car, I nudged the back gate open. I took a deep breath. I imagined myself as light as a happy sheep. Then I jumped down from the truck. I wouldn't claim that I was graceful, but neither was I injured. I was ready to make my escape. But I suddenly noticed that there were perimeter fences just inside the forest. How was I ever going to enter it now?

MARLON
(crow)

So, like, this cow is doing some major tool use at the back of this truck, right? And I'm saying to my bud, Jimmy D., "Hey, check it out!" And Jimmy D. is like totally into it too. So the cow opens the latch, and she pushes open the gate, and she jumps off, like it's some kind of prison break, right? And the human is a doofus; he doesn't even notice!

JIMMY D.
(crow)

It was totally, totally wicked!

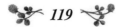

MARLON

(crow)

So true. But now the cow isn't moving, right? And I figure it's because of the fences, you know, because cows can't fly, which is a real drag. But I know where there's a gap she can get through, and I'm thinking maybe she and I can do some business, right, because that tooly thing would be awesome to possess.

JIMMY D.

(crow)

Owning it would be totally, totally wicked!

AUDREY

(cow)

The crow offered to show me a way into the forest in exchange for Buster's latch-catcher. In all honesty, I had no reason to hold onto it, and I would likely have just dropped it on the ground anyway. But it was clear that he saw some use in possessing it, and if the trade allowed me to get some critical information, then all the better for me. I was just about to agree when the car drove off, honking a warning about my escape. This was quickly followed by angry shouts as the driver rushed toward me. I was so close to gaining my freedom, so close that I could taste it, as they say. How could all the planning and effort and sacrifice by so many animals be stopped short now at the cusp? It was unfair. I wouldn't allow it. I quickly negotiated the terms of the exchange. I said to the crows, "If one of you can keep him busy while the other one takes me to the gap in the fence, *then* you have yourself a deal."

MARLON
(crow)

It was, like, bonus! We get the tooly thing *and* we get to annoy a human? Deal on!

KASEY
(human)

Jumpin' June bugs. You want to know why I made the switch to hauling furniture and appliances instead of cows and pigs? I'll tell you why. One: possessed farm animals. Two: a cow that magically opens latched gates. And three: a crow attacking my

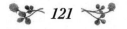

head to the point where I had to throw myself under Red Bessie to keep from having all my hair plucked out. That's why!

AUDREY

(cow)

And so, my first step into freedom required some deception on my part. It wouldn't be the last. The crow led me a short distance down the road to where a portion of fence was crushed flat by a fallen oak. Carefully, delicately, I picked my way across the mangled barrier, hopped over the tree using the skills I had honed a year earlier, and then walked past a curtain of ferns and low branches, finally slipping away into the dark, unknown forest.

THE HUNT

4

AUDREY

(cow)

First breath . . . softer
Second breath . . . deeper
Third breath and fourth breath
Freer and freer
Each breath a new breath
Each breath my own
Each breath a whisper
Of a future still unknown

It would be misleading to suggest that I composed this thoughtful poem right after my escape. Oh, no. In reality, my state of mind was quite the opposite. I was not thoughtful in the least. To put it mildly, I was a cow gone crazy. Giddy and elated, I giggled like a little calf, the way I used to when I was young and Eddie would tickle my nose with a bird feather. Freedom. I was woozy with it. All my worries? Gone. All my sadness? Gone. Imagine the spectacle. Me, in a big forest for the very first time in my life, completely hysterical with joy!

And then, well . . . my feelings shifted. Just like that, giggles turned into guffaws, heavy and loud. They shook my body. They thundered. They echoed around me, as if to declare "Audrey is here! Audrey stands proud and defiant, afraid of nothing! Afraid of nothing! Afraid of . . ." (*sigh*) My emotions changed yet again. Laughter suddenly turned to tears—not full of pain, mind you, or sorrow, but tears of exhaustion, tears of relief. The noose around my neck finally came undone, and I could really breathe again. "Mother," I said aloud, "I did it. I really did it."

TORCHY

(*human*)

I came onto the cow caper at five minutes past midnight. For a reporter like yours truly, a story doesn't get much better than Audrey's. But I didn't know it at first because I came late to the party. See, I'm busy chasing leads on the big bank robbery in Metro when I get a call from Tom. Tom? He's the *Daily Planet*'s senior editor. "Torchy," he says, "drop the bank heist and get yourself down to Grover's Corners double time. We've got a hot scoop, and it's melting fast." A hot scoop *where*? "Listen, Tom," I yelled back. "What kind of lousy hand are you trying to deal me here?" Without missing a beat, Tom says he's got a cow story he wants me to cover. So now I'm wondering if Tom has gone soft in the head. "What are you, bonkers? Have you flipped your lid? A cow story? That's the wackiest thing I've ever heard!" Don't get me wrong about Tom; I love the lug, but I wasn't born yesterday.

AUDREY

(cow)

My time for celebration was over. I needed to get away from the road if I hoped to make this freedom last. Well, I got my first taste of what the forest had in store for me. I'd never walked through brambles and broken branches before. They cut my legs and scraped my belly. And there were so many trees. Never-ending trees! I'd only ever rested under one tree, the big oak at Bittersweet Farm—a cool oasis on a hot day. But I'd never been under so many trees at the same time. They were extremely tall, with long limbs. I was tiny in comparison. I felt like one of Little Girl Elspeth's plastic toy animals that could fit in her palm. I was walking among the legs of giants. To those trees, I was nothing more than a speck, barely worthy of notice.

TORCHY

(human)

"So what cow story is getting better odds than a bank robbery in broad daylight?" I asked Tom. He tells me that Kent, a junior reporter, was at a place called Connie's Good Times Grill, which just happens to be down at Grover's Corners. It's karaoke night, and Kent starts chatting with a jumpy guy with a few too many root beer floats under his belt. Kasey is his name; he's an animal mover, see, the Grim Reaper's delivery boy. He takes cows and pigs to the slaughterhouse to be turned into steaks and cutlets. He's a cow's worst nightmare. But it seems the tables got turned. This luckless goofball tells Kent that he lost a prisoner in transit. That's right; some cow flew the coop, skipped town and ditched her date with destiny. Can you believe it? There's a cow in a forest, desperate and running for her life, and come morning, there will be a hunting party hot on her trail. Now *that's* a story!

AUDREY

(cow)

Yvonne of Bavaria slipped into the forest never to be seen again. That's how the tale ends. There are no additional chapters, no sequels; in fact, there are no words written down at all. But how I wished it had been otherwise. How reassuring it would have been to learn what Yvonne did afterward. Perhaps I could have used her actions as a blueprint for my own escape. *The Perilous Adventures of Yvonne of Bavaria*—both a story and a how-to manual for farm animals on the lam. But there wasn't. So I continued on blindly, without any particular direction.

The land was hilly, although not high or impossible to climb. I was attracted to any rise because I could see sky peeking between the tree trunks. I craved open space. But it was always an illusion. The hills were no less covered in trees than the lower parts of the forest. What I did begin to notice, though, which proved a beneficial discovery as far as my poor legs and hooves were concerned, were thin lines of beaten-down undergrowth that suggested pathways. They must have served a thinner animal than myself, but I was grateful for even that slight comfort.

JUNE

(deer)

We heard her longtime before we seen her. But we knowed that whoever it was, it weren't no forest creature. The way she stomped through them trees, snappin' twigs and all, she might *jes* as well holler her location to every *ki-yoot* or cougar in the neighborhood. I was stumped. We deer had done created a fine network of useful trails. Why on earth would you avoid them to bushwhack instead? Went on for hours. Spooked the young'uns, 'specially Doris.

AUDREY

(cow)

Eventually, the sun began to set, and the darker the forest grew, the clearer I could see that I didn't belong there. How could I have ever imagined that I would fit within those surroundings? How would I survive? I was unsure of what to eat. I noticed half-chewed leaves along the trails from time to time, but the plants were unfamiliar to me; I didn't know how they might affect my digestion or, worse, whether they would poison me. Then the sky grew overcast, and the wind picked up. Tree trunks scraped against each other, creaking slow and ominous. Pinecones dropped with the gusts. The ones that fell close startled me, prodding my imagination and quickening my heart. I was terribly afraid. My stomachs were twisted in knots. It was difficult to breathe. And then the rain began. Cold, fat drops. I stood there ankle deep in the underbrush, wet and shivering in the wind, too afraid to lie down, and wanting so badly to be back at Bittersweet Farm, warm in the cowshed with Eddie and Madge and . . . oh, how I missed Mother that night. How I needed her to be close, to reassure me that everything would be okay.

BORIS

(skunk)

The forest can be cruel. It's filled with hateful types and uppity sorts. There are the ones who turn their backs on you, and there are the ones who shut their eyes to avoid what's unpleasant. They're all the same in my book. And let us not forget evil. Oh, yes, the forest holds that too. . . . *(sigh)* She looked so pitiful. Miserable and pitiful. I am not one to get misty about such things, but to see that young lady all alone . . . my, my, my, sobbing and frightened, exposed to the elements, her head jolting about at the slightest sound, and her as plain to see as a bear cub in a snowstorm. Pitiful. Tugged at my heartstrings, she did. Played sad, sad music somewhere inside old Boris. . . . Thought I'd forgotten the melody long ago.

CLAUDETTE

(cougar)

Not in my nature to kill anything I haven't tasted before. But it is in my nature to be curious. Never seen a creature like her. Looked pretty stupid just standing there in the open. Could smell her fear all the way from where I was bedding that night, even in the downpour. I stalked her some but didn't attack. Stupid doesn't mean she won't still put up a fight. Needed to check her out some more. Thought maybe she was a moose at first. Heard stories of cougars taking down moose. Moose are big animals. More meat than on a deer. That girl was no moose though. She might have been big enough, but she had no antlers. And moose aren't so stupid.

DORIS

(deer)

I had bad dreams that night. Oh yeah! I kept seeing the shadow of some scary, gigantic monster-blob-a-ma-jig stomping through the woods, making those exact same crashing sounds we kept hearing the previous afternoon and evening. I could only imagine what kind of face a thing like that would have, you know, with a thousand sharp teeth and claws longer than a crow's beak. And it would be slobbering, with its tongue hanging low. Right? So I'd wake up all jumpy, and Mama would tell me to hush because she's fed up with my way-over-the-top imagination, as she puts it, and so then I'd go back to sleep and have the same tootin' nightmare! Oh yeah! It was an endless cycle of trauma that I can only hope will not scar me for life. But in the morning, we browsed the Red Maple trees and the Witch Hazel, and for a while I heard none of those spooky sounds, which was just fine with me. A fawn wants to eat her breakfast in peace. She doesn't want no crazy monster-thing sneaking up on her while she's nibbling on shrubs. Oh yeah!

AUDREY

(cow)

I didn't sleep a wink that first night. I was grateful to see the first orange streaks of dawn smudged across the sky. I counted my blessings. I had survived and that was something to acknowledge and be grateful for. Before I left Bittersweet Farm, Roy told me that I should be on my guard. He said that there are creatures other than humans that a cow has to be wary of in a forest. So, as I said, I managed to get through one night, and it gave me a little bit of confidence, even though I was near starving. It was my hunger that gave me the will to keep moving. My muscles were stiff and cold, and the effort was not without pain. But every now and then, I came across thin puddles of water that had not yet drained into the earth. I lapped them up with deep delight. That was my morning: moving from one puddle to the next but keeping an eye out for something familiar to eat.

KASEY

(human)

Jumpin' June bugs! My troubles were far from over after the flat tire. The cow disappeared into the woods and was gone in a flash. Once I got Red Bessie up and running, I had to tell the folks at Daisy Dream Abattoir that I had lost the cow. I tried explaining about the crazy farm animals, the cow opening the latch and the sudden crow attack. Mr. Ophal, the manager, checked my forehead for a fever! Then he refused to pay me or Bittersweet Farm for an undelivered cow.

So I phoned Bittersweet Farm. Glenn was none too thrilled either, don't you know, insisting the deal was done once I left his property. Words were flying, and I feared that they were going to make *me* pay for the cow! But when emotions finally simmered down, we all decided that we should notify the authorities, so that if worse came to worst and the cow wasn't found, the insurance company couldn't claim we didn't at least try to find her. Calls were made, plans discussed, and I'm shuttling between Daisy Dream, Bittersweet Farm and the regional police station, filling out reports and getting razzed by every officer on duty.

By the end of that day, I was as miserable and sorry as a man could be. I headed over to Connie's Good Times Grill, ready to drown my sorrows in root beer floats and country music. I find myself sitting next to this guy who starts asking me about karaoke night. I was in no mood to answer questions. My nerves were frayed! But when he sees I'm down in the dumps, he lends me a sympathetic ear, and the next thing you know, I'm telling him the whole crazy saga. Of course, I'm expecting him to break out laughing at any moment, just like everyone else. But no, he's real interested. He's asking me questions. "What are you going to do about the runaway cow now?" he says. I tell him that the police have called in some forest ranger or something, and he's going to track down that animal first thing in the morning. "And then what?" the guy asks. "And then what?" I repeat. "And then I'm going to get that darn cow over to Daisy Dream Abattoir and be done with the whole mess!"

Well, the guy just sits there thinking quietly for a minute. Then he pulls out his phone and calls his boss. He's relating my whole story, including the part about the cow hunt, and it's slowly dawning on me that he's a reporter. "No, no, no," I'm screaming at him. "You can't be reporting this!" He says, "Why not? You didn't say it was off the record." So you want to know the reason I moved out of Maple Valley? I'll tell you why: it's having every man, woman and child within a fifty-mile radius read in the newspaper that you were the guy who lost a cow because you were too busy hiding under your truck, from a crow.

JIMMY D.

(crow)

Is that what happened afterward? Oh, man, that is so totally, totally wicked!

HUMPHREY

(human)

Hmm? Just speak into the microphone? Starting whe— oh, now? Ahem . . . *AHEM!* *(cough, cough, cough)* . . . I AM AND HAVE BEEN A WILDLIFE ENFORCEMENT OFFICER FOR— What was that? Too loud? I see. . . . Ahem, let me start again.

I am, and have been, a Wildlife Enforcement Officer for well onto nineteen years . . . Better? . . . Very good. To continue . . . I received word of the cow in question from my supervisor, who phoned me at my home the evening of the escape. In my capacity as a Wildlife Enforcement Officer these past nineteen years, I have, among many other duties, been assigned to hunt problem bears, cougars, coyotes and such. But up until that point, I had never been ordered to track down a domestic bovine runaway. I was not well-versed in the behavior of cattle gone wild. However, I didn't foresee much difficulty in this assignment. As it was already dark, and I was deeply committed to the football game I was watching on television, I suggested to my supervisor that I retrieve the cow first thing in the morning. I anticipated no more than a half day's effort at best.

When I arrived at our offices the next day, I was somewhat surprised to find a Miss Torchy Murrow waiting for me. She identified herself as a reporter for the *Daily Planet* and insisted on accompanying me in the search. I explained that in order to perform my job, there could be no interference from civilians. I would be carrying a rifle, albeit using tranquilizers rather than actual bullets, and would not want any mishap to occur should the cow in question attempt to bolt. Miss Murrow was not dissuaded. I then proceeded to explain that it was against department policy, which to be honest was not true, and that, besides, she was not dressed appropriately.

TORCHY

(human)

This frowning palooka in his spanking-clean uniform is telling *me* I ain't got the duds for duty. Well, I nearly blew my stack then and there. I said, "Listen, mister, I've hiked through city sewers in a skirt and open-toed heels! You think I'm going to shirk from a patch of mud and a few fallen leaves because I'm sporting a dress and an uptown hairdo? Get used to me, Forest Copper, we're so hitched together on this hunt, we'll be sending out wedding announcements by the afternoon!"

HUMPHREY
(human)

Well, yes, I did let her accompany me. I, uh . . . ahem . . . Miss Murrow, you perhaps have noticed, is a very persuasive individual.

AUDREY
(cow)

When Buster was studying the map back at Bittersweet Farm and searching for the best place for me to escape, I had no idea that the patch of green on the paper translated into so much forest. My morning was no different than the first day. I pressed on and on, following the web of trails, moving forward but without any sense of getting anywhere.

I was hungry and discouraged. For the first and only time, I considered giving up, walking back to the road—if I could ever find it again—and waiting to be picked up. It was foolish thinking, I admit, and it embarrasses me even now. Had I not been wallowing in self-pity, with no regard for the heroic efforts of all my friends at Bittersweet Farm, I'd have noticed earlier the swath of light behind a row of trees in the distance. And this time it wasn't atop a hill but straight ahead on flat ground.

I approached with caution, not so much in fear of danger, but in an attempt to curb my hope and not be overly disappointed. There was no need. As I neared, I discovered a beautiful meadow dotted with the blues and reds and yellows of wildflowers! I gasped. "Mother, do you see?" I whispered. "It's paradise. I've found Yvonne of Bavaria's hidden paradise." I half expected to see Yvonne herself, grazing on a patch of clover. She wasn't, of course. But when I did step into the open field, which was deliciously thick with grass, and felt the full force of sunlight wash over my body, I soon discovered that there was someone else.

BORIS

(skunk)

Two-leggers are infrequent visitors to our parts. The number of times I've observed them could be counted on the claws of but three of my four legs. In each case, they came into the forest with one purpose only. They were predators like Claudette, stalking their prey and killing it with shiny sticks that make loud bangs. Two-leggers carry out what they catch; they don't eat it then and there. Strange hunters, they are. I don't believe they hear very well, or smell or see well either, for that matter. My, my, my, two-leggers are a feeble sort. They rely on tracks. And scat. Maybe they've got other tricks, but if they do, I haven't figured them out yet. But old Boris has a few tricks under his fur too.

HUMPHREY

(human)

As a professional Wildlife Enforcement Officer, I have maintained standards of performance higher than most. I was not willing to compromise the quality of my work in order to accommodate a member of the press. So I excused myself, telling Miss Murrow that I needed to gather supplies for the hunt and promising to return shortly. In actual fact, I left the building through a back door, snuck around to the front and stealthily slipped away in my truck. After a few navigational errors, I arrived at the reported location of the cow's escape.

Surprisingly—although less so now, in hindsight—I was greeted by Miss Murrow, who had managed to finagle the truck driver's report from our office clerk and was waiting by the side of the road with two coffees. I refused her gesture at first, concerned that it was a bribe. However, as the coffee was still hot and smelled strongly of . . . well, excellent coffee, I felt that in an effort to maintain good media relations for the department, I should accept the peace offering. Ahem. Shortly after that, I got to work.

Cow tracks were evident, both outside the border fence and inside as well. They were not hard to spot; therefore, as suspected earlier, I didn't foresee any difficulty in pursuing the animal. Only her removal from the forest might be tricky, should she prove stubborn upon capture. I had my rifle at the ready to tranquilize her if necessary, which

in turn would allow time to radio in for support. What I
didn't anticipate was that after a half hour of following
very clear and obvious tracks, they would suddenly and
inexplicably stop.

BORIS

(skunk)

My, my, my, that's crazy talk. Impossible for big ol' animal
tracks to suddenly stop. However . . . should a tree branch
full of leaves be dragged along a trail several times over, it's
possible for those tracks to be erased. Heh, heh, heh.

TORCHY

(human)

You should have seen the bug-eyed peepers on Humphrey!
"What's buzzin', cousin?" I asked, 'cause suddenly we're at a

standstill, dead in the water, going nowhere fast. But Officer Stoneface wasn't saying a word. He's searching the ground like he lost a contact lens. "Tracks have stopped," he finally mumbles. "Tracks have stopped!" I yell. "What do ya mean, the tracks have stopped? She's a cow! What'd she do, hoof it up a tree?" Oh, this was rich. Audrey had learned to levitate. Or maybe she was abducted by aliens. Or maybe the hunted had just outsmarted the hunter. Humph thought he had it easy on this assignment, but hold your horses, the cow just pulled a Houdini! The ol' Disappearing Bovine Trick! I couldn't wait to file my report. Headline: *Small Town Cow Outwits Authorities. The Hunt Continues!*

HUMPHREY

(human)

Hmm? Yes, I did have the misfortune to read Miss Murrow's account of the first day's pursuit. Her writing style is somewhat colorful for my taste. And I take offence to the expression "Grumpy Humphrey the *Mild*-life Enforcement Officer." For the record, I am able to smile and have, on more than one occasion, laughed mirthfully.

DORIS

(deer)

It was like a vision! When she stepped out of the woods into the meadow, she was radiant. Oh yeah! I mean that. Her hide was shimmering golden and creamy. It was something amazing to behold, like when I dream of being grabbed by a giant hawk that swoops down and then carries me high where I can see forever—see Mama and the family below—and everything is peaceful and serene, and the hawk doesn't eat me in the end? Yeah, amazing to behold like *that*.

And big? That girl was crazy big! She was so big and beautiful, and her eyes were soft black like night sky and her scent was strange and glamorous, so I knew she was no monster. Mama would call me a fool for being so trusting. But I wasn't scared. I just had to meet her. Oh yeah! So I did. I walked across the meadow right up to her. "What are you?" I asked. She says, "I'm Audrey. I'm a Charolais, and I come all the way from France by way of Bittersweet Farm. And what are you?" I was speechless, was what I was. She talked in such deep tones, I could feel it rumbling in my chest. "I'm Doris," I finally managed. "Mama says

I'm a handful, and I come from the woods by way of that trail over there."

CLAUDETTE

(cougar)

Kept an eye on her all morning. Fear smell had gone by then. But still—lapping up puddle water? Too stupid to take the clear stuff from the river or pond nearby. Then she spots the meadow. Whole new scent comes off her. Childlike. Pleasant, even. It was joy. I was sniffing joy. Joy in the forest and too stupid to sense me on her trail. See her grazing like a deer. See her talking with a deer! She's prey. I knew she was prey. Slow and stupid with plenty of meat. I can take this thing, I thought. It will not be hard. Would have taken her too, then and there, if I hadn't been distracted.

BORIS

(skunk)

No one bothers old Boris much. Suits me fine. I prefer a wide berth. If all the forest folk are so afraid of getting "contaminated" in my presence, why should I give a rabbit pellet's worth of concern for their company? My, my, my, the world is a cold place. Not that any one of them would do more than shun me. I'm not big or particularly dangerous, but they know what I am capable of if cornered. I act the part too, mind you; play up the crazy so they aren't willing to chance it.

Even Claudette gives me a respectful distance. She and I nearly rubbed shoulders on our visitor's second day. I'd just finished wiping the trails clean. I was studying this peculiar young lady who calls herself Audrey, this creature that stirs old-time feelings inside me. I was studying her from a few paces back, hiding at the edge of Homestead Meadow. Seemed Claudette was doing some surveillance too. She caught wind of me. Gave me the sneer that serves as her smile. Didn't come any closer, though. She said, "Boris, your eyes are a whole lot bigger than your stomach if you're thinking of making that thing dinner."

I looked right back at her. "That thing has a name, Claudette. She's a Charolais. Guess you hadn't figured it out yet, for all your fancy stalking." That set her back on her heels. Claudette likes to think herself the great hunter, but she's no risk taker. "Thinking of having a go at her?" I asked. "You don't want to mess with Charolais. They are vicious as wolverines and stronger than any animal in this here forest. I don't know why she's among us, but I sure wouldn't want to tangle with her." Now, at the time, I had not the slightest clue what a Charolais was or was not capable of doing. The young lady looked kind and gentle. I just wanted to buy her a little time before Claudette's stomach grew bigger than *her* eyes.

AUDREY

(cow)

Doris was my first forest acquaintance. She looked as delicate as a dandelion seedpod with her small brown and white-dappled body perched on thin, wispy legs. I thought she might float away on the slightest breeze. Once she got over her shyness, there was something familiar in the way Doris bounced about while she talked a mile a minute, so fast I couldn't keep up half the time. She reminded me of Eddie when he was a pup. And I suppose she reminded me of myself too, telling me of her dreams and nightmares as vividly as if she were still in them. Doris could have been a younger sister, and it gave me pleasure to think of her so. I grazed contentedly while she babbled on, enjoying the sensation of eating the grass as much as tasting it. Each tug and chew of blade was acknowledged. Each swallow, a solemn moment of gratitude as my long stretch of hunger came to an end.

JUNE
(deer)

Needs *jes* a second out of my sight to get herself all mixed up in no-good, my Doris. Once stuck herself on a rock cliff, tryin' to explore a nest. Sneaked her foolish self onto a porcupine

too, pretendin' she be a ghost, and got herself a snoot full of quills for her efforts. Now this. Had I seen what she was doin' back there in Homestead Meadow, I'd have put a stop to it before it began. I would have avoided the meetin' ever takin' place. But like I said, with Doris, all it takes is but a second.

AUDREY

(cow)

Doris led me across the meadow until it dipped, and I saw not one but a whole group of deer grazing. In unison, the heads raised, but I easily guessed which of them belonged to Doris's

mother by the stern look on her face. We neared at a pace set somewhere between Doris's excitement and my hesitation. I tried to disarm her mother with a polite introduction, as Mother would have encouraged me to do. I managed no more than "How do you do? My name is —" before she cut me off.

JUNE
(deer)

I said to her, "I know what you are, girl. I've done heard accounts of your kind from family lore. Different color, mind you, but you still fit the bill. Your type lives within the fences, with them two-leggers. You don't belong here, do you?" I said, "*Do* you?"

DORIS
(deer)

I did not know why Mama was being so mean and cold, treating Audrey like she was dangerous or something. I tried to explain to Mama that Audrey was alright and we didn't need to worry about her even if she was different from us. In fact, Audrey wasn't all that different, because her and me, we discovered we ate the same way and that our stomachs were almost the same too. Oh yeah! I tried to tell Mama that, but she just hushed me up.

JUNE
(deer)

"No, ma'am," she answered. "This isn't where I belong. It's just that I have nowhere else to go." Um-hmm, *jes* as I was supposin'. But then, this here Audrey, she done explained her situation. I swallowed a heavy lump, hearin' her tale. That poor girl had barely outgrown her childhood and yet she was carryin' woes heavier than a turtle with two shells. I had nothin' personal against Audrey. I could see right from the get-go that she was no direct threat, which is why I let Doris indulge in her foolery. But only up to a point. Audrey might have been fine in manner and scent, but that don't mean she weren't dangerous. A big, passive creature like her has got herself a target on her hide. I didn't want Doris close by when the howls and growls made their move. I said, "You are welcome to graze and browse with us durin' the day. Come nightfall, we part company. You may not bed with us. If you survive until dawn, you may join us once more. And if durin' the day there is trouble, we won't wait for you. Is that understood?"

AUDREY

(cow)

I said, "Yes, ma'am." To be honest, I was very surprised to hear her talk as if danger was lurking just around the corner, because other than my active imagination and Roy's warnings, I had not encountered anything that I found life-threatening. But I wasn't one to argue with my elders, and I was grateful to have any company in my new forest life. As for where to bed at night, that problem was literally solved right then and there. Doris's family continued grazing, and as their progress took them over a small rise, suddenly I saw buildings at the far end of the meadow. I gasped in astonishment because before me was Bittersweet Farm.

Only it wasn't Bittersweet Farm, you see, it was another farm, complete with a small house and barn and fences, but all in terrible disrepair. It must have been abandoned many, many years earlier. Grass and weeds grew right up to the doorstep. The house might have been a cozy and cheery place in its prime, a place for a child like Little Girl Elspeth to feel content in, staring out the window toward the meadow on a cold, frosty morning. But now the remaining bits of red paint were faded, the chimney had crumbled and the roof had caved in toward the middle. It was as if the house had given up trying to pretend it was still a home and had sighed so intensely it broke itself and finally collapsed.

As for the barn, it was no more welcoming. It too was much smaller than what I had known, with a low sloping roof. Trees had grown right against the wood-slatted walls, and moss and ivy covered the shingles like hair, hanging over the edges in unkempt tresses. The barn door was pushed inward, held askew on a single, bent hinge. I squeezed myself through, feeling as if I was forcing myself into the dank, dark mouth of some long-sleeping creature. I half expected to be chewed and swallowed at any moment.

Inside the barn, I was pricked by a dozen narrow shafts of afternoon sun that poured through the many holes in the roof. I was intrigued by the strange patterns they created. But holes also meant that the roof offered little in the way of protection from the rain. I took a moment to consider whether this broken-down dwelling could be my new home. It was not ideal, that was certain. It was neither comfortable nor comforting. But I only needed some protection in the night, so I decided it would suffice.

DORIS

(deer)

It was all good! Mama let Audrey be family with us, and I got to show her all the different plants she'd never seen or tasted before. And that girl can eat. Oh yeah! I showed her the pond and the river where the water is cool and tasty. I showed her the best trails and the warmest spots to rest. And Audrey told me about Bittersweet Farm, Eddie and Buster, the lake called Atlantic, and the place called France where we decided we would go together and taste the clover and meet all her cousins.

When twilight came, which is when my jitters always get the best of me on account of the silent snatchers that roam the midnight woods, Audrey would nuzzle and lick my ears with her crazy big tongue. She'd tell me happy stories that I could take into my dreams so I could sleep better. Then she'd say good night and head over to Homestead Meadow to bed in her barn. Before I closed my eyes, I always wished really hard that Audrey would be okay and survive the night, so that I could see her at dawn the next day.

HUMPHREY

(human)

I continued to hunt for the cow for several days. I also continued to be accompanied by Miss Murrow, or Torchy, as she insisted I call her. Each morning I would encounter fresh bovine tracks that confirmed the animal was still alive. But consistent with the first day, her trail would simply end for no reason. Remarkably too, whereas I had expected to find what civilians often refer to as "cow patties," I discovered none whatsoever. Nor was I able to smell evidence of any, due to an almost unfailing cloud of skunk odor that hovered above the trails.

Contrary to what . . . uh, Torchy wrote in her daily news reports, I was not frustrated or befuddled, nor did I ever throw down my Wildlife Enforcement Officer cap "in a fit of utter exasperation." That would have been highly unprofessional. I was not put off by these setbacks, as I am a patient man. I was most willing to continue in the pursuit of the cow on my own. However, due to the growing public interest in the story generated by Miss . . . by Torchy, my supervisor felt that a larger team of officers could end the hunt more quickly.

TORCHY

(human)

Poor Humphrey-Dumphrey. Come day four, his boss is chewing his ear off, demanding results double time, or threatening to demote Ol' Humph to a guard at a petting zoo. I felt for the lug, I did. But as a reporter, I'm rooting for the gal fighting for her life. Did I milk the story? You better believe it, sister! I knew I had to slant this tale in the cow's favor, see. The readers needed to put themselves in Audrey's— that was her name, you know—Audrey's shoes. Not that I'm saying she was wearing a pair of loafers, but I wouldn't put it past her. That gal had pizzazz and plenty of moxie. We've all been there, see; we've all been backed into a corner with no place to go.

But stop the presses! Audrey was a story that wouldn't go away. Four days running, not a sign of her. I'm thinking if the cow keeps it up, I'll have a two-week series, and maybe it will even go national! Round five takes a twist, though. Now I'm following a half dozen officers into the woods, each one of them more stone-faced than the next. Heck, Ol' Humph was starting to look like Chuckles the Clown by comparison!

AUDREY

(cow)

Nights in the barn were never pleasant. I had no hay to soften the ground, and the air was stale; I felt like I was stuffed away in a musty old box. It was the opposite of freedom. The sky stayed clear and the moon was waxing. Its light seeped in, sometimes cross-hatched across my flank, like fence chain, hemming me in even more. Those were the loneliest times.

Back at Bittersweet Farm, I'd have drifted off to sleep with the hushed voices of Madge, Greta and the other ladies in my ears. Now, there was nothing soothing, nothing familiar. So I would make myself remember as vividly as possible all of the friends I had left behind. I'd think of Eddie and Buster and Roy. I was squeezing drops of comfort out of my memories the way Farmer squeezed water from a wet rag. There was Eddie running and barking with joy. There was Buster, his little eyes twinkling at a newly filled trough. Squeezing and remembering, squeezing and remembering until I could wring out a small smile. But memories are double-edged. They may warm you with happy thoughts of what you once had, but knowing you no longer have them leaves you cold, shivering and alone.

The fifth night was different. The fifth night was the worst. I heard sounds from outside, close to the wall. Padded steps with the faintest rustle of grass, controlled breath, a smack of lips, and then I saw a shadow projected onto the dirt floor. It was of a tail, rope-thick and long. I stared, near hypnotized as it slowly coiled and uncurled, while behind me, a voice growled low and soft as a lamb's ear. "Been watching you, Charolais," it said. "Wondering if you're dinner."

I jumped to my feet and turned, catching sight of two fierce amber eyes peering in between the slats of wood. In a

split second they were gone, as if I had imagined them. But I didn't. I could feel menace encircling the barn. I tried to keep track of the stranger's whereabouts, constantly shifting my position as she resumed prowling, first one way and then the other. "Hear you're dangerous, Charolais. Are you dangerous? Smelling fear now and, *mmmm*, that makes me so hungry. Wondering about you, Charolais. Wondering . . . but close to deciding."

She was out of the moonlight's reach, which meant she was nearer to the door, which foolishly I had always left open. "Why should I be afraid of you?" I asked, attempting a light, breezy quality to my quivering voice. "We've never met, and I could not imagine you would mean me harm." While I spoke, I walked as quietly as I could manage toward the door. I listened for any twig snaps or breath exhales. Then silence fell upon the barn as deafening as a roar. Intentions were clear; the time for waiting was over. I saw a fan of whiskers caught in the moonlight, barely extended into the doorway. With all my force I pushed against the door, casting out that yellow-eyed beast while catching a few of her whiskers in the doorjamb. She screamed and growled madly; strong, hard nails scratched and clawed at the wood. The pressure against the rickety door was formidable. She pounded once, twice, again and again. Oh, my, the threat was horribly clear: if I was to ever meet this creature in the open, exposed and unprotected, I would be no match for her at all. I *would* be her dinner.

THE ENDGAME

5

FAY

(human)

Like most everyone else, I was following the ongoing search for Audrey in the articles that Ms. Murrow wrote for the *Daily Planet* newspaper. The drama was so captivating; one could not help but root for Audrey. Her story was now more than just an amusing anecdote to e-mail to your friends. There was something universal in her struggle to remain free, something that touched each of us. But I could see the writing on the wall. It did not bode well for Audrey. With all the attention being focused on the story, and with each new day that Audrey remained free, the hunt grew larger. The Wildlife Department was looking foolish, so they had to end it. They wanted the story dead. In the meantime, I began making inquiries.

GLENN

(human)

Oh, yes, we were kept well-informed regarding the Audrey caper as it progressed. I was in touch with Kasey and the folks at Daisy Dream through daily phone calls. However, my youngest daughter, Elspeth, was particularly caught up in the story as told by that *Daily Planet* reporter, who seemed intent on turning Audrey into some kind of folk hero. Elspeth insisted on reading every news report out loud at the dinner table. And the way Roy, her horse, was regularly sticking his head in through the kitchen window each evening, you'd think he was trying to catch the latest information about Audrey too. I'm joking, of course, but on several occasions I

did find that a bunch of animals had gathered beside Roy near the window, something that I'd not seen before or since. Strange days: must have been that full moon.

I would say that by the end of the week the phone was ringing nonstop. There were requests for interviews and visits to the farm from television stations all across the globe. I said no, of course. It would have been too disruptive.

HUMPHREY

(human)

With more officers assigned to the task, my supervisor was certain that the cow, uh, that is to say Audrey, as Miss Murrow insisted I refer to her by name, would be cornered and captured within the fifth day. This, as it turned out, was not the case.

Whereas earlier, when I would follow cow tracks that suddenly stopped without explanation, we were now encountering another curious set of circumstances. Not to say that we didn't still find cow tracks. Indeed, we found an abundance of cow tracks. It's just that the cow tracks we found did not stop . . . ever. In fact, whenever we followed cow tracks along a trail that hit a fork, we would discover that those cow tracks continued in both directions, as if, um . . . as if Audrey had suddenly split into two cows. And when we divided up officers so we could follow both sets of tracks, we would discover upon reaching another fork that the tracks had divided yet again. Many of the trails we followed ended up looping in on themselves. We were quite literally walking in circles.

TORCHY

(human)

So whaddaya know, Bobby Joe? Ol' Humph ain't the Dumb Dora I took him for after all. See, a half dozen wildlife officers were added to the mix, but they were still no closer to putting the net on that half-ton runaway. It was loony tunes, a joke and a half, I tell ya! Audrey was playing with those fellas like they were toddlers. Now you see her, now you don't. Did she go this way or that way, or maybe she's standing right behind you! If I was a betting gal, and I most *soitenly* am, I'd have said to put your money on that heavyweight heifer. Audrey's peekaboo strategy was beating the odds. She was outwitting and outlasting each and every one of them forest coppers.

LUCILLE

(beaver)

Okay, fine, I'll tell you what I know. Boris the Skunk, he approached me three days after word spread about this cow's arrival. He said, "Please, Lucille. I'd like your professional opinion on a particular matter." Okay, fine. I'm down with that. I'm not like all those other folk in this forest who stick up their noses at Boris, who find him repulsive, or who say he doesn't know his place. Who he is, what he does, blah, blah, blah, none of that is of any interest to me. You like him, you hate him—okay, fine, whatever. I could care less. You hear what I'm saying?

But he and I have history. Boris the Skunk once used his smelly "power of persuasion" on my behalf when a pack of wolves started making advances. So frankly, Boris is someone I was indebted to. You do hear what I'm saying, right?

So I followed Boris, and he took me to a spot along a deer trail where there was a muddy indent of a footprint. I'd never seen one like that before. It kind of reminded me of a pair of lips I saw on a two-legger who was rowing past my dam last summer. Whatever. "Is that from the stranger?" I asked. Boris nodded. Then he looked at me. "Do you think you could make me a stamp of that, Lucille?" He pulled a piece of wood out from under a nearby fern that he must have stashed earlier. Okay, fine, shouldn't be too hard. I figured an hour's work tops. After all, we're only talking about an oversized pair of lips. I gave him a nod and I added a toothy grin. I said, "A favor for a favor, Boris." Then I got to carving.

BORIS

(skunk)

Lucille is a master carver. I respect her work, and to judge the quality, you need only consider how long the two-leggers

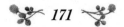

chased the phantom cow around the forest. . . . (*sigh*) I admit it was a lot of effort on my part, inventing a record of where Audrey might have been roaming. But that's alright. Old Boris doesn't sleep as well as he used to. I had time.

Now, the two-leggers were one thing; Claudette was another. I heard her screeches and growls echo through the woods that fifth night. I feared the worst for Audrey, but when I checked on her, I was relieved to see she was fine, although shaken. The next morning, I discovered five or six long whiskers on the ground by the barn entrance. And no sign of Claudette, neither that day nor the day after. My, my, my, poor Claudette. It would seem that her first encounter with a vicious Charolais didn't go as well as she hoped. Claudette was licking her wounds. But I knew she'd be back. And angry.

DORIS

(deer)

One morning we went down to the meadow to pay a social call on Audrey, but that girl didn't look too good. I'd say she was as white as a ghost, but that was her natural self already. Audrey was spooked, and as it so happens, I was too, on account of some horrible dreams I had the night before. There was a monster growling and screeching, and I was cornered, and Mama wasn't around to rescue me, and when I awoke, I just knew positively for sure that this time I had been emotionally scarred by my vivid and overactive imagination. Oh yeah! Audrey and I ate breakfast in silence that day. She was jumpy. She kept looking over her shoulder as if she might get attacked by my dream monster!

AUDREY

(cow)

How my emotions swung like a pendulum during my time in the forest—from the euphoria of escape to hopeless despair, then to happy optimism and back to unsettling fear. This was not the me that I knew and depended on. I was never so changeable, so erratic back at Bittersweet Farm. Perhaps I was a dreamer, but at my core, I was solid.

The truth was that after my midnight encounter with the velvet-voiced beast, I was quite simply unnerved. I was afraid of my own shadow. I began to have doubts about Yvonne of Bavaria's existence. Imagine! She was my guiding light, my hope and trust that there was a future for me in the woods.

How I envied Doris with her mother. I watched how June always kept a protective eye on her, but a cautious one on me. Where was *my* mother? Why was *I* orphaned? Fear was sapping my resolve. Toughen up, I would tell myself. Thicken your hide, Audrey. So I did, or at least I tried. I reminded myself of what there was to be grateful for. That I was still alive, still surviving. That I had a roof over my head and food enough to eat. That I had Doris and her family, and even if they weren't my family, I was allowed their company and perhaps, in time . . .

HUMPHREY
(human)

After three more days of being led on a wild cow chase, several things arose that caused me to reconsider the tactics we were using. First, Torchy's news reports went national, and that brought in television crews from all over. In general, they were a nuisance, and several more officers had to be brought in to keep them from obstructing our search. However, one

network had hired a helicopter to give their viewing audience a sense of scope, as they put it. The reporter in the helicopter claimed to have caught a glimpse of a large white creature in the woods that would certainly have fit Audrey's description. But where she spotted it was a fair distance away from where we were following cow tracks.

The second thing that was . . . unusual was that from time to time we would encounter animals and birds that would attack. What I mean is . . . we were not exactly accosted by wildlife but . . . there were occasions when twigs or pinecones were . . . they were dropped on us. I'm not suggesting that these creatures were trying to do us harm, but it did seem as if they were attempting to get our attention.

TYRONE

(badger)

Finally! It's about time someone asked our opinion about that Audrey problem. So how did the rest of us forest creatures feel about her living among us? We hated it! When she came into our neighborhood, she brought trouble along with her. We had two-leggers patrolling through the woods all day,

every day. You couldn't
step out of a hole or climb
down from a tree without wondering if you might get stomped
on. Then their flying doohickeys came swooping low over the
treetops, terrifying the bird folk, sending everyone scurrying
for cover. Don't get me wrong. I have nothing personal against
cows. I don't care for them, but I don't wish them any harm,
as long as they live where they're supposed to live and stay
away from our neighborhood. Riling up Claudette didn't do
us any favors either. That cow was disruptive to our way of
life. We have work to do, you know, and bellies to feed.

THELMA

(squirrel)

Hmm, how should I put this . . . cows are not like us. They're
different. They have different ways of going about things.

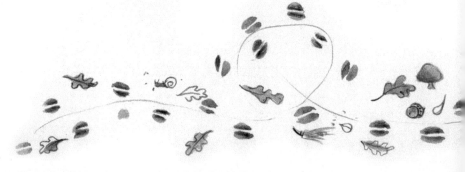

They're grass eaters,
for one, and although
I, personally, find that thought repulsive, maybe someone else wouldn't mind so much. But please, the whole cud chewing thing? That's just very, very off-putting. And I don't think I'm being out of line saying that, right? If one of my children was invited over to a cow's place to eat—I mean, to, you know, *re*-eat? Uh-uh, no way, that isn't going to happen on my watch.

Really now, we're expected to be tolerant, I know; we're expected to be understanding. But what about them? How come they can't make a little effort to be more like us? Why can't they eat like us? I'm not saying I would send them all to that Abbot's whatever to be killed, but then again, we only have Audrey's word on that, right? Is there really such a place?

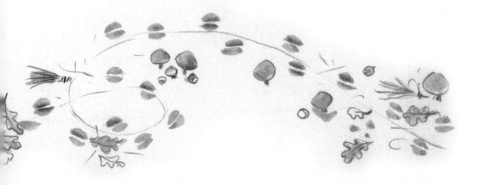

She could have been making it all up, to get our sympathy. She's a cow! She's different! Lying might be in her nature. We didn't know what was going on in her head. We didn't know if she had some, you know, ulterior motive. Maybe she'd done something bad to the two-leggers, you know?

I'm just saying, maybe they had good reason to catch her. Maybe she was dangerous. Maybe she carried a disease. Who knows what she was capable of doing. Was I supposed to stick my neck out for her? Was I supposed to let her cause trouble in *my* forest? I've met a few two-leggers in my time. They pass through. They look nice enough. I've heard they sometimes leave a nut or two lying around. I don't know why Boris was all about saving Audrey. It was reckless, I say. The smart thing would be to help the two-leggers. There could have been a reward. A nice bunch of free nuts would come in handy, you know? I'm just saying . . .

BORIS

(skunk)

They meddled! The Tyrones and the Thelmas and their like. *They* interfered! Cowards! Collaborators! Yes, you heard me!

Old Boris doesn't mince his words. Audrey came into our home desperate and alone, and we were obligated to help. They turned their backs on her, they colluded, they . . . My, my, my, how their paws are stained with guilt. (*sigh*) . . . It was over. I could no longer help her. I could no longer stamp the trails. Wherever I was, they would warn the two-leggers and bring attention to my whereabouts. I had to rush. I had to constantly hide. Finally, I stumbled. Barely escaped, and left the stamp behind. It was too late to retrieve it.

HUMPHREY

(human)

On the eighth day, I came across a crudely made stamp of a cow's hoof. It was clear that someone had taken it upon him or herself to obstruct our search in an effort to keep Audrey from capture, or to make the Department look foolish, or perhaps both. What was also now clear was that we were looking in the wrong part of the forest. I studied the maps and discovered a likely location for Audrey to be living, assuming that the helicopter sighting was accurate, and that she was still alive after all this time. Let me add that as a professional Wildlife Enforcement Officer, I find no amusement in childish pranks.

TORCHY
(human)

Don't look at me, sister! I may add a few colorful adjectives to the mix, but I'm a newshound to the bone. I just report the news; I don't make it myself.

BORIS
(skunk)

I had failed. I heard the two-leggers talking. They knew where to go now. I had to warn Audrey.

GLENN
(human)

Kasey phoned me at dinnertime, shortly after the search entered its second week. The Wildlife Department had a new plan, he said. He then explained it to me. I didn't like it. But I agreed to assist in the hope of putting a stop to all the phone calls, and the reporters sneaking onto the property.

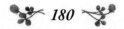

Kasey said he'd be by with the truck just before dawn the next morning.

MADGE

(cow)

Oh, we weren't scared. We knew exactly what the truck was all about, plain and simple. Since the day after Audrey left, the whole farm was following the events. Eddie taught himself to fetch the paper from the mailbox at the end of the drive each afternoon, and then drop it down at Little Girl Elspeth's feet just as she got off the school bus.

Poor Eddie was so desperate to know Audrey was alright, so eager to learn if she had eluded those hunters another day. But then, so were we all. A lot of the animals couldn't even wait for Roy to make the rounds. Those who had the freedom to move about, or were able to convince Buster to open their gates, would head over to Farmer's house and stand under the kitchen window to hear the latest. We were all rooting for her, even Norma; even Max, I suspect. So when Farmer came and got me and Agnes that morning and loaded us up on the truck, we knew why we were being taken—okay, maybe Agnes was a bit confused—but I knew, and I was not happy about being used as an accomplice in Audrey's capture.

CLAUDETTE
(cougar)

Nasty creature, Charolais. Nasty and vicious. Ruined my face. Talked of friendly meetings, and then ruined my face! Vicious creature. But still stupid. Still prey. Hunting her would be a pleasure. No more caution. No more waiting. Stupid Charolais was going to be my dinner. And after I took her down, I was going to eat her slow.

AUDREY
(cow)

When I look back, I can say that I made the best of things. I can say that I even found moments of small joy. I spent my days with Doris and her family, learning more and more about the forest and observing the creatures that made their life under its leafy canopy. If I stopped to listen, I could hear a symphony of sounds around me. From above, there were warbles, twitters and love songs. From the pond, there were croaks, peeps and trills. From the burrows and brambles, there were chitters, squeaks and hisses.

All these languages were new and unfamiliar, but my ears grew accustomed, and quickly I could make out a word here or phrase there. I discovered how truly universal our conversations are. "Let us look for food together." "Did you see what the so-and-sos built their nest with?" "How I love a sunny afternoon."

The desire to jump right in and add my thoughts to these easy, breezy exchanges was hard to resist. But I continued to be polite, as Mother had raised me to be, and I attempted a hello only if I deemed it safe. I cannot say that my greetings were returned in kind. I suppose I was still viewed suspiciously, as a stranger. Some scurried away in fear while others, I felt, were outright hostile to my advances. I kept reminding myself, in time they will see that I mean no one any harm. In time.

And in the evenings, I would help put Doris to bed, telling her gentle stories to ease her into sleep. But when her mother gave me a curt nod, I would return to the meadow on my own. Back into the darkness of the stuffy, broken barn, remembering to always push the door closed and lie against it, to prevent any more attempts at entry by unwelcome guests. My nights were not pleasant, and I courted sleep by imagining a bigger barn full of all the cows I had known and cared about, eavesdropping on their gossip and complaints and jokes until sleep finally overtook me. But on the eighth day, on a rare occasion when I was in the meadow all by myself, I was met by a creature that up until then I had not seen.

BORIS

(skunk)

She did not back away when I approached. For an animal like old Boris, much used to seeing expressions of revulsion, it was both a surprise and a pleasure to be greeted with genuine civility. I introduced myself. She responded accordingly. "It's a lovely day," she said. "Yes, it is," I agreed. "I heard a birdsong this morning," she offered. "One that I had not noticed before. A series of sharp whistles—*peerda, peerda, peerda*. Very pretty. Do you know who it belongs to?" "Sadly, I do not," I replied.

We continued on in this fashion, turning those few short moments into a waking dream. Old-time feelings washing over me like floodwater. I was engaged in polite conversation, as I had always wished for and imagined: me and a young lady discussing the simple details of a summer day, comparing observations, laughing at the vagaries of forest society. My, my, my, I could have, at any moment, wept tears. Oh, how cruel to taste the happiness I had longed for my whole life, yet knowing that I must end it. I had to. Time was of the essence. "They are coming for you, dear lady."

My sudden shift in tone startled her. "Who are coming for me?" she asked. "The two-leggers," I explained. "The predators. I've tried my best to keep them at bay. I've used all the tricks that I have at my meagre disposal, but I fear I have failed you." Her face sagged, but she did not crumple. I suspect she had experienced similar news in the past. "You say that you've been protecting me?" "Yes," I replied, "from your first night in the forest, when I spied you alone in despair." I went on to explain all my ruses. She nodded slowly; for a moment, she was lost among thoughts no doubt turbulent.

But then her eyes softened, and she looked at me—she *looked* at me and smiled. "Thank you, Boris. Thank you for allowing me these days of freedom. Thank you for granting me days of life that I would never have had otherwise. Thank you." And this time I did weep. How could I not? This child, this beautiful child . . . yes . . . I wept. She came over to me, leaned down and nuzzled my fur. "It's alright," she whispered. "It's alright, Boris. It's over. I'll prepare myself to meet them."

What? Surrender? "No!" I shouted. "What I mean is, no, that's not what I—I mean, you must get away, not give up. I have contacts. Trustworthy, as far as such creatures go. I will ask them to help. Yes! They will smuggle you out!"

AUDREY

(cow)

"Smuggle me out? But to where?" I asked him. "Where else is there for me to hide?" Boris was insistent that I not lose hope. "This forest is vast, young lady. It stretches beyond the two-leggers' roads. You'll see. But getting away will be difficult if they are looking for you. It must be done under cover of darkness. There are professionals who can guide you. I'll arrange for them to escort you this very night. Be ready. Please, be safe." And then Boris, who had been my protector all along, who nobly and secretly kept me safe for no other reason than out of the decency of his dear, dear heart; that generous yet ferocious soul took his leave as humbly as he had come to me.

I stood alone in the meadow, wondering what was to happen next. Could I continue on to someplace else, a place without a clearing or barn or Doris and her family? How could I carry on without any of these things? How could I possibly make a home elsewhere?

Then I looked at the house at the far end of the meadow, collapsed and rotten, hollow and sad, and I laughed at my foolishness. I had no home. I was only pretending this was a home, the way Little Girl Elspeth served imaginary tea to her dolls when she was smaller. Homestead Meadow was not Bittersweet Farm. My nights were spent in a cage, not a barn; and they were populated, not with real friends and family, but only with memories of them. And Doris, as much as I had grown to love her like a sister, could not be my sister if my presence might lead to her harm. I had to move on. I had to believe that there was a home for me somewhere out there.

Evening was approaching. I headed into the woods. I needed to tuck Doris in and say my good-byes, and then wait for Boris's friends.

OLIVER

(raccoon)

Righty-right, Boris and us go way back. Can't get into the particulars, mind you, because—and stop me if I get too technical—one is beholden to the statutes of limits regarding laws upheld in certain places and jurisdictions. Ipso facto, any discussion might be deemed as a confession of sorts. So you might say we'd be self-incriminating ourselves, if you follow my train of thought. Ask Stan if I'm correct in my summation.

STAN
(raccoon)

He most certainly is, my Oliver.

OLIVER
(raccoon)

Righty-right, there you go. But to the point: if something needs to be smuggled in or smuggled out, Stan and me, we're the ones to get the job done. As to the job in question, we

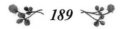

were to pick up a "package" at the far end of Homestead Meadow a couple of owl hoots past midnight.

DORIS

(deer)

Audrey gave me an extra-long story time that night, full of funny bits involving Eddie, who is a creature called a dog but sounds awfully like a wolf, and Buster, who I don't even know what he is. And there's this bird called a rooster, who can't fly but has to holler every dawn, which I would personally find too stressful because a fawn needs her mornings quiet. Oh yeah! I loved Audrey's stories. That girl could spin a tale like no one else. And after she said "happily ever after," then we both recited the poem she made up just for me.

My forest bed is veiled and soft
It keeps me safe, it keeps me sound
I close my eyes and gently sleep
Toward my dreams I now am bound

JUNE
(deer)

I was hard on the girl. I suppose I was afeared to let her into my heart, in case I might make reckless decisions. In the forest, you only get yourself but one chance. But on that evenin', after she tucked Doris in, I took her aside. I told Audrey that I wished her luck and happiness on her long journey. I told her she was a good girl and that her Mama would done be proud to have such a kind and courageous daughter. Weren't much to say, but I felt it was somethin' important for her to hear.

HUMPHREY
(human)

There was an old abandoned farmstead deep in the forest that I discovered in some old maps we had on file back at the office. It belonged to the Doolittle clan, an early pioneer family. Standard tracking methods were getting us nowhere in this hunt. What was required was to get into the head of a cow, to think how a cow thinks, and figure how she might cope in her new environment. That is what led me to the conclusion that the old farm was where I'd find Audrey. Whatever cleared fields there were had likely grown over decades ago, but the general layout of the farm might be familiar to a domestic bovine. To make it irresistible for Audrey, I decided to plant some decoys to lure her in. And then, like a duck hunter waiting in a blind, I would set up a position on the edge of the clearing, ready to take her down just past dawn.

CLAUDETTE

(cougar)

Not in my nature to hunt in daylight. Make an exception for stupid Charolais. Can't take her when she's in her barn-cave. Wait for her to come out. Wait silently at the meadow edge. Wait for morning to break. Then I take Charolais down.

TORCHY

(human)

The Audrey escapades were reaching the end, see. Ol' Humph grew all steely-eyed and determined, the hunters were closing in, and the curtains were about to come down

on this show. If that brave bovine had another ace up her sleeve, this would have been the time to play it. Sure, I wanted the story to continue. I got a job to do, but then, I suppose, so does Ol' Humph. But had I a minute alone with the lady, I'd have told her to scram, to beat it, to hit the road.

AUDREY

(cow)

I sat in the barn half the night waiting for my escorts to arrive. My senses were so sharp that I was alert to every sound, sight and smell that a forest offered. Hour upon hour, my range broadened: the owl hoots, the cricket chirps in the meadow, the frog choruses from the nearby pond, the distant howls. Breezes prodded tree branches and grasses, making their shadows dance and bow. Breezes also brought the heavier scents of moss and mushroom that I ignored during the day, in favor of the flower perfumes that I prefer. But now the flowers were asleep and unconcerned. So I waited and waited, yet did not tire. How surprised I was to hear the scraping and whispers of those two fellows, who had somehow managed to enter the barn undetected, despite my vigilant attention.

OLIVER
(raccoon)

Well, of course she didn't hear us slip in. We're grade-A, top-notch professionals, we are, and as such, me and Stan possess the qualities of stealth and cunning that allow for sneaky movement. It would hardly do, to be picked off by "the package" prior to arriving at the rendezvous. Ask Stan if I'm correct in my synopsis.

STAN
(raccoon)

He most certainly is, my Oliver.

OLIVER
(raccoon)

Righty-right, then. So, upon meeting "the package" at the aforementioned place as specified by our old and dear friend, Boris, a.k.a. "The Skunk," we were immediately smacked in

the face by two details. Details that, as pertaining to the successful hush-hush transportation of goods, would be significant problems.

STAN
(raccoon)

She was huge and white!

OLIVER
(raccoon)

Indeed she was, indeed she was. Righty-right, then, we got ourselves a smuggling liability. Can't perform any easy alterations in the size department, if you follow me. But as pertaining to the bright color adorning "the package," making undetected travel difficult if not impossible, me and Stan reached into our wily bag of craftiness and came up with an inspired plan for camouflage that did the trick, if I do say so myself.

STAN
(raccoon)

We covered her in mud, we did!

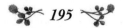

OLIVER

(raccoon)

Always to the point, my esteemed colleague Stan, always to the blunt point. But yes, indeed, we plastered "the package" in a covering of moist dirt attained from the bank of the nearby pond. Our scheduled time of departure was appreciably set back, as you can imagine, on account of the sizeable "canvas" we were working with. To take advantage of whatever darkness was still available, we needed to move fast if we were to reach the far side of the forest before dawn.

AUDREY

(cow)

They wanted me to bushwhack through the forest in near total darkness, and they wanted me to do so at a hurried pace. I couldn't see as well as they could, and I was neither small enough nor agile enough to keep up. "Stop," I finally said. "This will not do. At this rate, I will break a leg. Find me another route." My escorts were not pleased with my demand, but even they could see that it was reasonable. There was a wide path marked by two bumpy furrows that led away from the meadow. I had been warned by Doris's family to never walk along it. After some debate between Oliver and Stan, we shifted our escape route to that path, even though it was not as safe.

OLIVER

(raccoon)

The first rule of smuggling is to avoid all routes that offer two-leggers ample access to your personage. To put it another way, if they can see you, they can catch you. As such, the route we were forced to use, which at one time served to connect the Homestead Meadow to the more often used two-legger road, was a big, red-flag no-no.

But righty-right, "the package" made her argument, and the sun was itching to rise, so I said to my Stan, "Stan," I said, "our options are few and fraught with challenges; we are tormented by conditions undeserved. The forbidden two-legger road, on this occasion, offers our only salvation. But let us take comfort in the fact that this thoroughfare is long past its practical days, and the likelihood of anyone using it is near to nil." That is what I said. Ask Stan if I am correct in my citation.

STAN
(raccoon)

He most certainly is, my Oliver, word for word.

OLIVER
(raccoon)

So, righty-right, off we go, traipsing down the long-abandoned, weed-infested, barely-a-shadow-of-its-former-self two-legger road, and you'll never guess what happened. But take a guess anyway, just for a bit of fun.

 *198*

KASEY

(human)

Phew, what a day that was. I went over to Bittersweet Farm with Red Bessie around four-thirty in the morning. It was dark and cold, and I was in no mood to be dealing with any crazy animals, don't you know. Glenn Parker was already out there in the open area beside the cowshed with two of them sneaky creatures and his sheepdog. Glenn isn't talking to me much, on account of the whole Audrey thing, but them two cows were calm and cooperative, not dancing or anything, and that's all that mattered to me. We loaded them up the ramp onto Red Bessie, Glenn gets into the passenger seat, and we head off.

AUDREY

(cow)

It was much easier using the abandoned road. I still had to be careful because the furrows were uneven and rocky, requiring me to be sure of each step before pressing down. But as dawn approached, the dark lifted slowly until I could safely mark the route. Of course, no matter how fast I went,

I was never fast enough for my escorts, who grumbled out loud almost continuously, only stopping to shush *me*, who wasn't saying a peep. We were very close to reaching the main two-legger road when suddenly both my escorts stopped talking, stood up on their hind legs and shushed me again with more urgency. They had heard something, and a moment later, I heard it too.

OLIVER

(raccoon)

So have you had yourself a little guess yet? Have you figured out what happened to me and dear Stan and "the package," who insisted we take the easier route? I'll give you a little hint. The second rule of smuggling is that if anything, even something a whisker's breadth away from impossible, has the possibility of happening, then more than likely it *will* happen. Keeping this in mind, what do you think we could possibly have come across, while going our merry little way along an all-but-forgotten, nothing-to-have-a-worry-about, abandoned two-legger road?

STAN
(raccoon)

We saw a truck, we did!

OLIVER
(raccoon)

Took the words right out of my mouth.

KASEY
(human)

I had my map out because I was instructed by the Wildlife Enforcement Officer to take the cows to some long-forgotten field somewhere in the middle of the forest, and the only way to get there was by an unmarked service road. Forty-five minutes of driving and we're getting close. It's lighter outside but still not daylight, so we nearly miss the turn. But Glenn thinks he sees it; he points and shouts. I take a sharp right, and jumpin' June bugs, I plow Red Bessie along the bumpiest road imaginable. Barely a half second in and my bouncing headlights catch two raccoons frantically pushing what looks like a giant black boulder off to the side. Now,

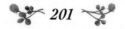

other people might find that weird, but after what I've seen, nothing really surprises me anymore.

OLIVER

(raccoon)

Righty-right, we hear a noise, and it doesn't sound too friendly. Me and Stan, professional smugglers that we are, break into evasive maneuvers. I turn to "the package" and I shout, "Duck!"

Sadly, my unfortunate choice of words confuses both "the package" and Stan, who immediately begins to look for the waterfowl in question. I try again, yelling, "Hide!" and pushing "the package" off to the edge. Because with only a second to spare, a hideously large and loud vehicle was coming barreling down the never-ever-used road and straight at us, promising extensive damage to our persons upon impact. I shout out for a third time, returning to the very fitting verb "Duck!" yet again. This time, my partner Stan takes my point, and following my example, throws himself to the ground, allowing the truck to pass over our terrified and wobbly but still-in-one-piece bodies.

AUDREY

(cow)

I knew the sound of that truck as soon as it came into ear-shot. You don't quickly forget the contraption meant to take you to your demise. After it rocked and bounced past us, snorting and belching like some angry bull, I lifted my head, and to my horror, saw Madge and Agnes hanging on for dear life in the back. It was both alarming and confusing. Why were they in the Abbot's War truck? They were milk cows, and there was no reason to take them . . . unless it was some kind of punishment, to teach the other animals a lesson per-haps because . . . because of me.

Were they being punished because I escaped? But why take them to the meadow? Is that what they did with milk cows? Did their lives end there instead of at Abbot's War? None of it made any sense. But my eyes met Madge's, and they looked so scared. I took a step back onto the road, and she started to bellow. They drove off toward the meadow, and soon she was too far away for me to hear what she was say-ing. But it couldn't have been good. I was frantic. Meanwhile, my escorts insisted we continue across the road up ahead and carry on to the other side of the forest. But what about Madge and Agnes? I couldn't just abandon my friends in their time of need, especially if their trouble was my fault.

MADGE

(cow)

I saw her. It was Audrey; I was sure of it. I recognized her dear face and soft eyes. But her hide was so blackened and cracked, I thought perhaps she was ill. Then she got up and moved toward the truck, so I bellowed a warning. As she receded behind us, I yelled, "Stay away, Audrey! It's a trap! Stay far away!" In moments, we were out of view. I didn't know if she had heard me, but I wished so deeply that she had.

OLIVER

(raccoon)

Righty-right then, the two-legger vehicle was out of sight, out of mind. I checked my limbs—all accounted for—and Stan's self-appraisal reached the same conclusion.

Up on our feet, we're breathing fine, life is good, time to get back to work. Our destination is but a few dozen steps

away. We need only deliver "the package" across the smooth road yonder, point her in the right direction, and our contractual obligations with dear and old friend Boris, a.k.a. "The Skunk," is a foregone conclusion.

So take a small stab of speculation at what happened next. How do you think "the package" rewarded all our hard labor? Care to have a go?

STAN
(raccoon)

She done run back to the meadow, she did!

OLIVER
(raccoon)

It's enough to make a grown raccoon cry.

AUDREY
(cow)

I galloped back toward the meadow, pushing and exerting every muscle in my body, as I imagine Roy might have done in his younger days. I was reckless in my pursuit of that truck, crossing the same demanding terrain I had cautiously tread earlier, but now at quadruple the speed. I didn't care. I just knew I had to get there. I wasn't even sure what I would do when I did.

CLAUDETTE
(cougar)

Waited behind her barn-cave since sunrise. Came ready to hunt and kill. Heard two-leggers walking nearby in the forest. Didn't care. Only cared about stupid, vicious Charolais. So quiet in her barn-cave. No fear-smell this time. Not any smell. Began to wonder if Charolais was there. But I knew she was. She was always there, stupid, vicious creature. Heard two-legger vehicle coming into meadow. Didn't care. Not interested in two-leggers. Only interested in Charolais. Only interested in ripping her to shreds and teaching her a lesson.

TORCHY

(human)

Why sure, I could *tell* you what happened next, but for a more vivid account of the blow-by-blow action, I suggest you read my story in the next day's paper.

AUDREY'S QUEST FOR FREEDOM ENDS IN MAYHEM

By Torchy Murrow
Special to the *Daily Planet*

This infamous day began well before daylight, dear readers. While the stars still twinkled in the bruised, purple sky, yours truly met up once again with tall, rugged Officer Humphrey. We stood along a lonely stretch of highway bordering the vast forest that one brave and wily cow named Audrey has called sanctuary for over a week. Steam curled up from the cups of coffee that Officer

Humphrey and I drank in silence; a solemn moment before what was expected to be the final chapter in our heroine's story.

With his square jaw firmly set, Officer Humphrey slung the rifle over his broad shoulder, flicked on his trusty flashlight and led this reporter through a tangle of trees and rough terrain toward a concealed location. As we entered, the noisy woods went eerily still. I felt as if all eyes were upon us, bird and animal alike, watching our furtive movements and waiting for events to play out.

Clean-shaven Officer Humphrey and I huddled close together in our small, secreted roost. We looked out onto an open meadow that, if things went according to plan, would serve as the stage for this drama.

Surely as night turns to day, the dawn broke and night turned to day. At 5:23, as per schedule, we heard the loud huff and puff of Red Bessie, the truck that many of you readers will remember as the one assigned to deliver our heroine to her death. On this cool, early summer morning, it was being driven by none other than Mr. Kasey Krumpfelt, the same hapless half-wit who lay hiding beneath Red Bessie, cowardly avoiding the overtures of a single crow, while Audrey made her escape. But this time, the truck was making a different delivery, bringing two milk cows from Bittersweet Farm to serve as lures to reel Audrey in.

It lurched to a stop in the middle of the meadow. Krumpfelt, along with Glenn Parker, the owner of the farm where Audrey grew up, left the truck and began unloading the cows. Whereas earlier, the cows were bellowing from what one might only imagine was fear, now they stood silent. Meanwhile, beside me, handsome Officer Humphrey furrowed his thick eyebrows in concentration. Something was afoot. Cool as a cucumber, he lifted his rifle and planted it firmly in the crook of his shoulder. Then I heard what he heard. A *thump-thump, thump-thump, thump-thump* as quick as my own excited heartbeat, but growing louder and louder. Something was coming, and coming fast.

It was Audrey! She rushed toward her fellow cows with the determination of a racehorse, dried mud breaking off her like the shell from a newborn bird. She came with fury, like a bullet, like a steam engine. Nothing was going to stop her, certainly not Kasey Krumpfelt, whose frantically waving arms were the last things I saw before he was bowled over. To my right, I heard the faint click of the cocked hammer. Officer Humphrey was taking aim. His arm was steady. His breath was measured.

Dear readers, I heard the shot. It echoed through the trees, sending birds scattering in all directions. But dear readers, I also saw, seemingly from out of nowhere, the powerful, muscular body of a cougar leap into the air, claws out and sharp teeth exposed, and land on our poor heroine's back, pulling her down hard into the long, wild grass. I feared, dear readers, that Audrey was no more.

THE AFTERWARDS

6

EDDIE

(dog)

I chased her off the farm and down the road on the day of her escape. I watched her standing in the back, so darn frightened, getting smaller and smaller as the truck sped up and my legs tired and slowed. Finally, I stopped running. (*sigh*) I turned around.

During my walk to the farm, I had my first real thoughts about Audrey not making it—I mean, jeepers, not just being out of *my* life, but actually being out of *her* life, not surviving. Gosh, imagine a world without Audrey. That would be the saddest world I could think of.

Then I remembered once asking Audrey's mom, when I was just a pup, where we all go when we're no longer here. "I don't know, Eddie," is what she replied. "I don't think any of us really know. Where do you think we should go?" I doubt I had an answer at the time. But while I walked back home, back to Bittersweet Farm, watching Roy sauntering over to the orchard and the sheep returning to their arguments and the cows already grazing and gossiping—the first hints of normal life settling in again—I did have an answer. I think that if Audrey shouldn't survive, I would like to believe she'd be somewhere similar to here, a place where she knew happiness. But this time . . . it would *only* be happiness.

BORIS

(skunk)

She came back! Why did she have to come back? Why give those two-leggers a second chance? Why give Claudette the opportunity, for that matter? Old Boris's heart was near to breaking when she went down. Guns and growls. My, my, my, the forest can be cruel.

DORIS

(deer)

Mama wouldn't let me go to Homestead Meadow during all the commotion. It was a nasty business, oh yeah! I woke up to the ugly noise of a monster chugging and belching, rumbling all angry-like. Then I heard achy moans and shouts that sounded almost like Audrey, but wasn't Audrey because I know that girl's voice. Then I heard growls. They were the nastiest—all high-pitched and sharp, they dug themselves right under my skin just like they do in my nightmares. And then there was this big *crack-bang*. Or maybe two, but I'm not sure because a fawn can't be expected to count under such traumatic conditions. Mama said it was thunder, but that was no thunder. Then there was just silence. No monsters, no moans, no growls, no nothing. I said to Mama we should have a look. I wanted to check in with Audrey to find out if she caught some of the action. Mama yelled, "No, Doris! You stay put!" Mama sounded crazy upset, but her eyes were scared, so I stayed put just like she said.

MADGE

(cow)

She was so brave, charging toward Agnes and me, her expression so determined. Farmer and the other might have thought themselves clever with their ruse, but Audrey was not walking mindlessly into a trap. She was rushing into the fire to save those dear to her. Even as I bellowed out warnings to stay back, I couldn't help but admire her heroism. And then that vicious animal coming out of nowhere, and those piercing claps that sent birds flying in all directions . . . and then

Audrey pulled down into the grass . . . her body so still, the claw marks and blood staining her hide . . .

Poor child, I whispered. Poor, brave child.

AUDREY

(cow)

The first thing I saw was sheep as white as clouds. Or were they clouds? I wasn't entirely sure. My head was so groggy and the sun seemed particularly bright, giving everything a halo glow. If they were sheep, they certainly were very happy sheep, I thought, bleating hellos and good wishes and assuring me that my troubles were over and I had found true peace.

TORCHY
(human)

If you bothered to read the rest of the article, you would have seen that I made a mistake, which I retracted in the follow-up. See, there were two shots, not one. Thought I was hearing the echo of the first shot, not realizing Ol' Humph has the reflexes of a cheetah.

AUDREY
(cow)

Then I saw a horse sauntering way off in the distance, but her gait was not even. She had a bad limp off her back leg.

HUMPHREY
(human)

Reflexes of a cheetah . . . that's what she said? No, no, I like that . . . a cheetah, sleek, fast . . . yes, I like that. But, um, to be, uh, serious, I didn't think, I just reacted. I had Audrey in my scope, and then, out of nowhere, this cougar crossed my line of fire. One does what one has to do. . . . She actually said a cheetah?

FAY

(human)

As is often the case with humans, it all comes down to money, doesn't it? The dispute between Daisy Dream and Bittersweet Farm and Kasey's Delivery regarding who was the rightful owner of Audrey, and who was owed or not owed payment, was an unpleasant issue I unfortunately needed to involve myself with. However, prior to talking to those gentlemen, I had already contacted some of our benefactors and laid out my proposal. I wanted to be prepared. I didn't intend to take no for an answer.

AUDREY

(cow)

There was a creature that I now know to be a donkey. His hide was broken in long ugly welts, and he had the saddest eyes I had ever seen. Marcel is his name, and I soon discovered that he composes love poems, always for Judy, who brays shyly before running to hide.

TORCHY

(human)

Aw, heck and applesauce, don't get me started, or I'll be turning on the waterworks again! I didn't want Audrey bumped off, story or no story. That gal was aces with me.

AUDREY

(cow)

There were so many animals and most, it seemed, had some problem or another. But all of them looked happy and content. What was this place, I wondered. It must be paradise, right? So where was Mother, or Madge and Agnes?

FAY

(human)

I made calls, and I used my contacts and connections. I even got hold of that reporter, Torchy Murrow. I told her what my intentions were, and she got all excited, perhaps because she

saw an ending to this story that might sell a whole bunch more newspapers. But on what she called the "hush-hush," she filled me in on the plan to use decoy cows to lure Audrey to a spot where they could take her down. After that, it was likely off to the abattoir again and good-bye Audrey, so time was running out.

Ms. Murrow told me where and when this would all take place. So the next day, I'm up before dawn, heading toward some unmarked service road and I—oh, by the way, just as a side note, I passed two raccoons sitting up on their hind legs, and I swear one of them slapped himself on the forehead, raised his two front paws in the air and rolled his eyes—anyway, I went down this bumpy road, and I hear a couple of gun shots. I reach the meadow and see a big red truck, two milk cows,

a dazed-looking man staggering to his feet and Audrey on the ground, motionless, with a huge cougar sprawled on top of her.

Something went wrong, I thought. I was too late.

HUMPHREY

(human)

Having fired my weapon and watched both Audrey and the cougar go down, I rose from my hiding spot, took out my binoculars and surveyed the aftermath. Satisfied with what I saw, I passed on my report to Miss Murrow, beside me, who took the information quite emotionally. The reason that I didn't get over to the bodies right away was because I was being . . . um, well, I was being forcefully held back by Miss Murrow.

TORCHY
(human)

Well, lock me up and throw away the key, sure, I kissed him! Why, I just had to lay a smooch on Mister Wildlife Officer after what he did! Ol' Humph shot his tranquilizer gun and put that cougar to sleep in mid-flight. He saved Audrey's life! If that don't deserve a reward, then this town is cheaper than a sock puppet's phone bill!

AUDREY
(cow)

I turned to one of the sheep and asked her, "Is this paradise? Is that where I am?" She replied in the softest voice, "No, that's not what it's called. The name is Sanctuary. Fay's Sanctuary."

FAY
(human)

And then the wildlife officer came over and checked on the cougar, who it turned out was as fast asleep as Audrey, for both of them had been tranquilized. Audrey had a few claw marks on her, but other than that, she would be fine.

The officer contacted his department to get assistance with the cougar, while I took my cell phone and called Daisy Dream Abattoir. When I got the manager on the line, I turned to Mr. Parker and Mr. Krumpfelt and told them why I was there: to demand Audrey's freedom.

I explained that I have a farm, Fay's Sanctuary, whose sole mission is to provide care and respite for animals that have suffered injury or trauma. It is a place where these animals can live out the rest of their lives in peace. Like many other people who had become aware of Audrey's plight through Ms. Murrow's articles, I had grown fond of and concerned for her. Audrey's story was strange and unusual. It seemed wrong to ignore the uniqueness of the events and send Audrey to the abattoir as if it had all been nothing but a glitch in the system. Audrey deserved more, I said.

As anticipated, their response was not like-minded; there was the issue of money and investment, etcetera, etcetera. But since I came armed with sizeable checks, their voices grew quiet, and the business of buying Audrey was resolved quickly and without too much fuss. I made another call and brought in a truck with a winch. We kept Audrey sedated so that we could transport her safely. We hoisted her gently onto a soft bed of hay and took her to her new home.

As for Audrey's room and board, once the news media reported that we would be providing a permanent home for her, small donations made by regular folk started pouring in. We now had the funds to be able to give her comfort and care for the rest of her life.

AGNES

(cow)

Okay, so, like here is what happened as far as I've been able to figure it. Me and Madge were chosen to take part in some kind of secret cow training mission. I know, eh! Like what's *that* all about? (*snort*) But I'm thinking it's on account of that spaceship I saw flying over the farm a while back. But then

Audrey shows up, and I'm like, "Whoa! No way! She must be running the operation, which is why she hasn't been around the farm lately!" And then this growling, furry space alien comes out of nowhere and attacks Audrey. There's blood everywhere, which is really, really bad but also really, really interesting because it's so gross. Oops. (*snort*) Sorry. But then all of a sudden both Audrey and the space alien get zapped by invisible freeze rays that turn them into lifeless statues. I know, eh! Did I hit the mystery jackpot or what! (*snort*) . . . Of course, Madge saw things a bit differently than me.

AUDREY

(cow)

When tempest tossed
When overwhelmed
When life is harsh and scary
Protect your heart
Until you find
A place called Sanctuary . . .

Sanctuary. I like that word. I like the chewy feel of it in my mouth when I say it. I like that such a word should exist. As for paradise, there was a twinge of sadness when I realized I wasn't about to see Mother anytime soon. More troubling was not knowing what happened to Madge and Agnes back at the meadow. If they weren't here, safe with me, then where were they? But eventually my worst fears were put to rest when a visitor came by with news.

GLENN

(human)

My daughter, Elspeth, announced at dinner a few days after the capture that she wanted to go see Audrey and make sure she was alright. I assured her that the cow was fine, but Elspeth wasn't satisfied. She stood on her chair and insisted she needed to see Fay's Sanctuary with her own eyes. I admit that I was a little curious myself. So I promised Elspeth that I would drive her there on Sunday morning if she agreed to sit down and finish her meal. I heard a whinny coming from Roy through the kitchen window, which seemed to seal the deal for her. Come Sunday, we head over to the car and

Eddie, our dog, was already there waiting in the front seat, as if he knew where we were going. So the three of us headed over to Fay's Sanctuary.

EDDIE

(dog)

Gosh, I don't know where to start. It was all so wonderful and exciting, like a surprise gift. Madge and Agnes came back to Bittersweet Farm bursting with news about Audrey— about how heroic she was running to save them, the cougar attack, the gunshots, and finally about Kind Lady Fay who offered Audrey a new home. She was going to be alright; *alive* and alright! All of us sure felt swell about how things turned out. We felt proud too, because we accomplished something important. But when Roy heard about the ride over to Sanctuary, he came directly to me. Roy said, "You might want to mosey down to Farmer's motor vehicle come Sunday morning." Darn tootin', I would! Once he filled me in on what was happening, I knew that nothing was going to stop me from heading over to Sanctuary too, not Farmer, not Dad, not a tornado of sheep.

AUDREY

(cow)

Eddie flew out of that car like he had grown wings. I watched him tear across the yard in a blur of fur and a shower of yaps until I felt his cold nose next to mine. It was so good to see my friend again, to nuzzle him and lick his ears, to thank him once more for being my friend. Eddie came loaded with regards and assurances that everyone, Madge and Agnes included, was fine.

Then Little Girl Elspeth came over, gave me pats and kisses, and whispered her secrets while she stood on tiptoe. But when Fay's promise of cookies and juice pulled her away, I was able to show Eddie around and introduce him to my new family, so that he would have stories to bring back to my first family, my beloved family, the family I could never forget.

Saying good-bye to him yet again was difficult, but not nearly as hard as the first time. I could no more return to my life at Bittersweet Farm than I could pretend that I lived on a real farm when I was back in the forest. As much as I would have liked to return to my old life with Eddie, Buster, Roy and the ladies, in my heart of hearts, I knew that was impossible.

Bittersweet Farm was a working farm, and every animal had a job. My position, should I have come back, would still include a one-way trip to Abbot's War. So that couldn't be my future. And I suppose I won't be going on my clover-tasting tour of France either, although one still can dream.

I live at Fay's Sanctuary now. This is where I belong. I've made many new friends, good friends, like Marcel and Judy whom I've already mentioned, as well as Carmen, a cat that even Eddie would take a shine to. We care for each other here and help each other through our pains and discomforts, which are many, and through the fearful memories that haunt us and the sadness that sometimes crosses over us like a winter shadow. And when we feel joys, we don't hoard them; we pass them around, giving them a voice in song and poetry and nods of understanding. And when it is time to go, and for each of us there is a time, we all sit by the one who is leaving. We tell stories and share silence, both light and heavy, and we bid them a gentle farewell.

Goodness, the time! I'm afraid you must excuse me. Kind Lady Fay is bringing a new arrival this afternoon, and I'm in charge of the welcoming committee this month. I'd like to

thank you again for all your interest in my story. The attention has been very flattering indeed. . . . Oh, and it's a llama,
by the way. That's who we are expecting to join us. A llama.
I've never met a llama before. . . . I do hope they like poetry.

The End

ACKNOWLEDGMENTS

Acknowledgment must be given to one Charlene Mooken, otherwise known as Cincinnati Freedom. She was the inspiration for this story. Back in 2002, I read a news item about a thousand-pound Charolais cow that escaped the slaughterhouse near Cincinnati, Ohio, by jumping over a six-foot fence and running into a nearby wooded park. Charlene avoided capture for eleven days. SPCA officers and police set traps and shot tranquilizer darts to no avail. Meanwhile, newspapers, radio stations and television newscasts fed a growing audience of Charlene supporters with daily updates. It was only when three cows were used as decoys that authorities were finally able to apprehend her, but by that time, her popularity had grown to the point that generous offers were made to keep her from having to go back to the slaughterhouse. Charlene was dubbed Cincinnati Freedom, and was even given a key to the city. She spent the rest of her life at Farm Sanctuary's New York Shelter. And yes, there actually was an Yvonne of Bavaria too.

Special thanks also go to the humans that made it possible for this story to become a book, namely Hilary McMahon, Tara Walker, Debbie Rogosin and, of course and always, Mimi.